A DEVILIS

"Why didn't you tell Charles about last night?" Lord Deveril asked, his darkly handsome face lit by a mocking smile.

He was watching Christina closely, and smiled again at her silence. "Cat got your tongue? I can't blame you. It might be difficult to explain to your fiancé that you were kissing me in the moonlight."

"Then you tell Charles!" she snapped, and made as if to pass him. But he barred her way. His hand on her arm seemed to burn her, and she glared down at it.

He laughed and removed it. "You didn't despise my touch last night, as I recall."

"Last night was—a temporary aberration," she said. "A moon madness. It meant nothing and it will not happen again."

"Do you think so?" he said softly, hatefully.

"Oh, you *devil*!" she whispered, against her will.

DAWN LINDSEY was born and grew up in Oklahoma, where her ancestors were early pioneers, so she came by her fascination with history naturally. After graduating from college she pursued several careers, including writing romance novels. She and her attorney husband now make their home in the San Francisco area.

DEVIL'S LADY

by
Dawn Lindsey

A SIGNET BOOK

SIGNET
Published by the Penguin Group
Penguin Books USA Inc., 375 Hudson Street,
New York, New York 10014, U.S.A.
Penguin Books Ltd, 27 Wrights Lane,
London W8 5TZ, England
Penguin Books Australia Ltd, Ringwood,
Victoria, Australia
Penguin Books Canada Ltd, 2801 John Street,
Markham, Ontario, Canada L3R 1B4
Penguin Books (N.Z.) Ltd, 182-190 Wairau Road,
Auckland 10, New Zealand

Penguin Books Ltd, Registered Offices:
Harmondsworth, Middlesex, England

First published by Signet, an imprint of New American Library, a division of
Penguin Books USA Inc.

First Printing, May, 1991
10 9 8 7 6 5 4 3 2 1

To my sisters

Chapter 1

A MASKED BALL at Ranelagh Gardens drew the world and his wife. Elegant ladies, safely anonymous behind mask and domino, flirted outrageously with handsome cavaliers, for once quite happily rubbing shoulders with their social inferiors, all in the name of intrigue. Inebriated young sprigs of fashion ogled ripe females in their nearly transparent muslins, and the usual rigid decorum that marked most social events was noticeably absent. As the evening wore on, the rooms also grew hotter and more airless, silks and shirt collars wilting and tempers starting to fray.

A figure all in black stood out from this colorful throng, notable by his very air of detachment. He seemed to have come that evening for no other purpose than to prop up the wall with his broad shoulders and survey the crowd with unmistakable boredom, for he had yet to put himself to the exertion of dancing.

More than one bold damsel had eyed him with interest, struck as much by that indifference as by the undoubted elegance of the black figure and its profile seen behind the black mask. The more fanciful among them told themselves with a pleasurable shiver that he looked distinctly dangerous. But if asked to explain, they would undoubtedly have had to fall back on the vaguest of generalities: the blackness of his domino and mask, perhaps, and that general air of cynical amusement. And of course those eyes, so light a gray as to appear almost silver in his dark face. Unnatural they were, seeming to see right into your soul, and to express no interest in what they saw there.

They were resting on the noisy throng now as if scarcely aware of it, a mocking twist to that sensuous mouth.

Then, unexpectedly, the eyes narrowed for a fraction of a second. The next moment he lifted his black shoulders from the wall and strolled forward, his tall figure readily traceable by its height and distinction in the heat and confusion.

His destination seemed to be a couple at one side of the floor, near the doors leading out into the garden. They were engaged in some sort of altercation, for a slender figure in a blue domino with flaming hair was struggling with a red-faced man in green. He had her by the wrist and was attempting to pull her onto the floor. It was evident he had imbibed rather too freely, for he was laughing at her struggles and refused to release his hold on her.

No one near them seemed to notice, and it was doubtful they would have attempted to intervene if they had. Anything might happen at Ranelagh Gardens past midnight, and it was wisest to keep one's curiosity to oneself.

Then Black Domino had reached them. He tapped the red-faced man on the shoulder and said politely, sounding bored, "I believe the lady is promised to me for this dance."

Both figures in the struggle started and seemed to be equally astonished. The girl turned rapidly, revealing a delicate color and a pair of very dark blue eyes between the slits of her mask which at the moment were looking distinctly skeptical.

Her erstwhile partner was slower on the uptake. "Eh?"

he cried, slurring his words and growing even redder in the face. "Oh no, you don't! You don't steal such a prize right from under my very nose, blast you."

He still had not released her wrist. Black Domino yawned and put what appeared to be an indolent hand on the green shoulder.

"I repeat, the lady is promised to me."

He did not seem to exert any pressure, but of a sudden the red-faced man began to swear and abruptly released his hold. "Damme!" he cried, twisting to escape that oddly unpleasant grip. "This is highway robbery! You'll answer to me for this, you—"

Then he got a good look at his adversary for the first time and boggled, growing oddly pale where before he had been brick red. "Oh," he gabbled, beginning to sweat. "I had no idea—must excuse me. Just remembered something—" He almost fled.

Black Domino and Blue watched his scuttling figure disappear across the floor. After a moment the girl turned back, less gratitude in her glance than frank speculation. At close quarters her coloring was seen to be even more remarkable: her skin naturally pale, her brows dark, and her hair flaming in the light of the myriad candles. Her mask covered most of her features, but she was seen to possess a straight little nose, an unexpectedly willful chin, and a very kissable mouth.

"I believe I am in your debt, sir. Thank you," she remarked in a voice that was intriguingly husky.

Black Domino shrugged. "It was nothing. Did you know him?"

For the first time she betrayed some surprise. "No. Didn't you? From the way he disappeared, it seemed he was at least acquainted with you."

"I doubt it," he answered indifferently. "Shall I escort

you back to your party?'' He had a deep, rather drawling voice that betrayed his habitual boredom.

Again she was surprised and for some reason colored faintly. It seemed she had expected him to replace Green Domino's importunities with his own, and with better grounds to appeal to her gratitude. He smiled, well aware of it, and waited politely.

After a moment she recovered and said quickly, ''Thank you, but that won't be necessary. I have troubled you enough already.''

''But I insist. You should not be on your own in such a place. Who are you with?''

For a moment she looked almost annoyed. Then she made a vague gesture toward the other side of the room. ''Some friends. I fear I have temporarily lost them. Do you see a lady in a puce turban? Rather stout?''

He was taller than most of the crowd and so could easily see over their heads. As he turned to look, scanning the far side of the room for a lady in a puce turban, she hesitated only a moment, then deliberately slipped quickly away through the crowd of dancers.

He turned back just in time to see her disappearing through the doors leading out into the gardens.

He stared after her for a moment, his face unreadable. Then, with an expression that seemed to mock himself, he more leisurely followed her.

He reached the door as she stood poised on the top steps leading down into the dark garden. The *torchères* on either side of the door turned her hair to flame, making her easily recognizable. Then she picked up her skirts and fled into the night, her pale domino floating behind her.

Again he followed. For one so large he moved with unexpected silence, for she seemed unaware of his presence behind her. She plunged quickly down one of the paths leading toward the river, and seemed to know where she was going. Now and then a scattered lantern lit up her hair and figure, as if to provide a beacon for her pursuer, but she did not bother to halt or look behind her.

At length she reached a small pavilion tucked out of the way and overlooking the river. A fine river mist was rising, but the pavilion was dimly lit by lanterns and showed itself to be empty.

She seemed to have come to the same conclusion, for she halted and then exclaimed in annoyance, "Oh, the devil fly away with all men!"

Her pursuer laughed. As she turned quickly with a little gasp, he stepped into the light behind her. "What, abandoned, oh fair incognita?" he mocked her. "Perhaps you should not have discarded my protection quite so readily."

For a moment she shrank from him, and he belatedly realized that he stood silhouetted against the light, his shadow stretching in an exaggerated shape before him and his face in darkness.

He was merely amused by the aptness of the illusion, but nevertheless abandoned the shadows and came on lightly toward her, his dark domino thrown carelessly over his broad shoulders and his mask dangling now from his fingers.

"Well?" he said, "have you turned to stone, like Lot's wife? As I recall, she, too, made the mistake of looking back as she fled the evil behind her, and was instantly stricken where she stood."

There was a certain wariness in her expression, but she recovered her voice. "You seem not to know your Bible, sir," she replied somewhat tartly. "As I recall, Lot's wife turned to salt."

He bowed. "I stand corrected. I will confess the Bible is not my preferred reading."

When he said nothing else she seemed a little at a loss. "Why did you follow me, sir?" she demanded directly after a moment. "I believe it must have been clear that I wished to be left alone."

"Oh, quite clear," he agreed in amusement. "Which is precisely why I followed you."

"Why, this is vanity indeed," she exclaimed. "Are you so bored with conquest you must needs pursue where you are not wanted?"

He merely shrugged. "Have you not learned that no man can resist a mystery—especially at a masked ball?"

"Then I am sorry to disappoint you. I am anything but mysterious. The truth is, my shoes pinch, and I am longing only for my bed."

"I am desolated to be obliged to contradict you," he corrected, still in amusement. "Both those may be true, but you are definitely a mystery. I have been watching you most of the evening, and you are with no friends, in or out of a puce turban. You haven't gone near anyone, and have spent most of the evening trying to avoid the inevitable attentions you received from those like your late, unlamented partner. He was merely more persistent—or drunker—than most."

She achieved a quite creditable yawn. "Is that to flatter me, sir?" she demanded cynically. "As you can rightly point out, you are hardly the first tonight to swear that I am the most beautiful woman in the room and try to force his attentions on me."

"Oh, there were several women here tonight more beautiful than you are, Red," he corrected mockingly. "Your coloring is magnificent, and I confess I have myself always had a certain weakness for Titian hair, but at the moment you are decidedly out of fashion, you know. The current mode, I regret to say, is for simpering blondes. But from what I can see, your eyes are undoubtedly brilliant, but a little too widely set for real beauty, and your mouth by far too passionate.''

She seemed not to know what to make of that. ''Are you always this brutally honest, sir?''

''Only when it suits my purpose. I find that honesty, like most other virtues, is vastly overrated.''

''And what is your purpose?'' she asked bluntly.

''You needn't worry, Red,'' he said in amusement. ''At the moment, no more than to dance with you. I seldom make plans beyond that.''

''But then—according to you!—you might have done that any time this last hour,'' she pointed out.

''Ah, do you doubt me? Very well, I shall prove it to you. You danced once with a fair man in a crimson domino who trod on your toes, refused half a dozen other partners, and have since done your best to disappear into the wallpaper. You would have to wear a sack over your head to do that, I fear. Your coloring is by far too vivid to hide, even in a crowd. Am I right?''

She was regarding him with both astonishment and dawning amusement. ''About my coloring or my actions? You do indeed seem to use truth as a weapon, sir. I scarce know whether to be flattered or offended.''

He smiled down at her with unexpected warmth. ''For once no offense was intended. I have already confessed, have I not, that I have a partiality for red hair?''

''And then admitted you would not have put yourself to the trouble of approaching me had I not piqued your interest by running away.''

For once the habitual boredom in his expression seemed to be almost wholly missing. ''I am beginning to think you are the exception that disproves my own disheartening rule. I had almost given up on finding a woman of both wit and beauty.''

"I fear you flatter me, sir," she said politely. "Were you to meet me tomorrow, under ordinary circumstances, I have no doubt you would find me as hopelessly commonplace as you do most women."

His teeth gleamed briefly in the darkness. "Doubtless tomorrow we will both of us find the other a disappointment," he conceded. "But for the moment there is moonlight and an odd enchantment, and if you don't know it yet, that is far too rare to allow to slip away, believe me. Come, dance with me and let the devil take care of tomorrow."

"But I mistrust enchantment," she said frankly. "Unlike you, I prefer to have my feet firmly on the ground."

"Then you should not be here. Has no one told you that masked balls were created for taking risks?" When she still hesitated, he added tauntingly, "Or are you afraid to discover it may not be an illusion after all? That there is more to what lies between us than mere moonlight magic?"

"There is nothing that lies between us," she said a little too quickly.

"Then prove it." He held out his hand.

She seemed startled. "What—here?"

"Surely you don't prefer that hot and overcrowded room? At any rate, enchantment is best cultivated in the dark. And we both feel the enchantment, don't we? I will confess it is almost the last thing I expected to feel tonight, in this place."

Almost weakly she allowed him to take her hand and swing her into the dance. The sound of a waltz could be heard faintly in the background, and there was indeed an odd exhilaration in dancing there, with only a few faint lanterns to light them. The night air was cool and the silence vastly preferable to the overcrowded ballroom.

"You dance well," he remarked at last.

"No. I think it must be the moonlight," she said truthfully.

"You were right that there is a strange enchantment to it. I must remember that and be forewarned in the future."

"Are you always so cautious?" he asked curiously.

"I had certainly always thought myself so. You were right to warn me that masked balls could be dangerous."

Abruptly he stopped dancing, though he held her still within his clasp. "So I am beginning to see," he acknowledged. "In fact, I really think I must risk disillusionment after all."

Before she realized his intent, he had put up a hand to the strings at the side of her mask. She would have prevented him, but he was far too strong for her. He caught both of her wrists in one hand and held her while his probing fingers deftly untied the strings at her temple.

After that first effort at resistance she stood stiffly beneath his hands, only breathing a little fast. When he had succeeded in removing her mask, she met his glance and demanded defiantly, "Well? And are you disillusioned?"

He smiled, his dark face very close to her own. "Oddly enough, no. I almost think it would have been safer—for both of us—if I had been. You have a very kissable mouth, Red. Did you know that? And I really don't think I can resist it."

She had by now grown a little pale, but she made no foolish protests or pleas for mercy. "And what if I am disillusioned?" she countered as her final weapon.

He shrugged. "Why, that is a risk I will just have to take. If you are, it will be over soon enough, I promise you. And you'll undoubtedly survive the experience."

It was clear she could not avoid it, and so made no futile and undignified attempt to struggle when his hand turned her face up to his.

But when his mouth lowered and claimed her own, she resisted for the space of a heartbeat. Then she sighed, and her lids drifted down.

At least he refrained from gloating over his easy victory.

At her capitulation his arms tightened about her, and he threw up his head, as if in surprise.

When he kissed her for the second time, she made no resistance at all.

Only when a sound intruded behind them were they reminded of the outside world. He raised his head, regretfully it seemed, and after a moment he said in amusement, "Open your eyes, Red. I won't let you fall. But I fear we are about to be interrupted."

Instantly her eyes flew open, rage and disbelief rapidly replacing her earlier weakness. "Who *are* you?" she demanded.

He turned so that the light caught the unusual silver gleam of his eyes. "Some call me the Devil," he admitted, grinning. "But don't worry. I've not claimed your soul. Yet."

She shivered abruptly, and at the further sounds of impending approach she quickly recalled her scattered wits and drew herself out of his embrace.

She was not a moment too soon. "Kit?" demanded a petulant voice from somewhere in the darkness. "Are you there? Plague take it, I can't see a thing in this blackness."

"Kit," mused her companion regretfully. "I must confess I prefer Red."

But with the voice the last of the madness seemed to leave her. "Good God!" she exclaimed, her hand stealing to her flushed mouth. "I must have been mad!"

"Not mad. Merely moonstruck."

Abruptly he raised her left hand and stripped off her glove. "Ah, no ring, I see," he said in satisfaction. "I'll admit that marriage would have presented a slight obstacle, if not an insurmountable one. I take it the approaching—if belated— gentleman is not your husband?"

She snatched her hand away. "Good God, he mustn't find you here!"

He laughed and tucked the glove in the breast pocket of his coat. "Very well. He is clearly unworthy of you, but I will bide my time—for the moment." At the edge of the pavilion he paused. "But we shall meet again, Red," he promised her softly. "In fact, I will find you if I have to go to the bowels of hell to do it."

He laughed again and melted into blackness as a figure came hurriedly up the stairs. "Kit? Who was that with you?" the newcomer demanded suspiciously.

She seemed not to hear him for an instant. Then she shook her head as if to clear it. "No one," she said. "Did you get the money?"

"Lord, yes, though it took me half the night to track him down, curse him." He, too, was masked, and his eyes, very like her own, blazed with excitement between the slits of the mask. He seemed to see her for the first time and added in surprise, "What happened to your glove? Did you lose it?"

"Yes. I—I lost it," she said wearily. "For God's sake, let's go home. I discover I have had enough of masked balls. They are clearly dangerous."

Chapter 2

LORD DEVERIL was still completing his leisurely toilet the following morning when his good friend Mr. Charles Heybridge was shown up.

The latter, glowing with all the natural superiority of one who had been up since seven, took one look at his lordship's elaborately brocaded dressing gown, worn over his shirt, breeches, and elegant top boots, and exclaimed in disgust, "Good Lord, Dev! Aren't you dressed yet? It's nearly noon."

His lordship glanced up from paring his nails, the unusual silver of his eyes momentarily evident. "I fear I lack your disgustingly cheerful nature, Charles," he drawled in his habitual bored tones. He possessed a tall, powerful figure that not all his valet's efforts and his languid air succeeded in disguising. "But you should know I am never at my best before noon. I prefer not to inflict myself upon others, except for Lacock here, of course, who is paid to put up with my bad manners." He allowed himself to be divested of his elegant dressing gown.

The valet permitted himself a slight smile at this mild jest, and tenderly held out his lordship's coat of blue superfine. His lordship's powerful figure was coaxed into it, not without difficulty, and the valet stepped back to view the results with the discerning eye of a connoisseur. "Excellent, my lord! Excellent!" he cried enthusiastically. "The fit is just as it should be. Mr. Weston has outdone himself this time, if I may be permitted to say so."

Mr. Heybridge observed this delicate operation with all the derision of one who had known his lordship from the cradle. "Good God, Dev, you're starting to take this ridiculous reputation of yours far too seriously."

Lacock looked scandalized, but his lordship merely yawned. "I never take anything seriously, least of all myself," he said, accepting his quizzing glass from the ubiquitious Lacock and looping its black cord around his neck before disposing of the glass in his waistcoat pocket. "At any rate, lacking your manly beauty, my dear Charles, I fear I must make do with being fashionable. Have you come merely to scoff, by the way, or was there some purpose to your visit? I fear Lacock dislikes being disturbed in the execution of his delicate art."

Again the valet permitted himself a slight, perfunctory smile. "I venture to think I am equal to the challenge, my lord," he said, beginning to gather up the discarded cravats and his lordship's dressing gown. "Will you be needing anything else, my lord?"

"No, nothing. You may go. Stay one moment. Hand me my snuffbox first."

The little valet fussily did so, stopping to flick an invisible spot of dust from his lordship's gleaming Hessians before at last bustling out.

"Lord, Dev, why do you put up with him?" demanded Mr. Heybridge impatiently. "What a fool he is."

"Oh, indubitably. But he keeps my clothes in excellent order and he amuses me," said his lordship, stowing the snuffbox in one pocket and leading the way out the door.

"But I doubt you came around to discuss the follies of my valet. How have you been, by the way?"

"I've come to drag you off to lunch. It seems an age since I last saw you."

They were not very much alike. Charles was a fair, pleasant-looking young man of some thirty years of age, easygoing to a fault; whereas his lordship had the reputation of not enduring fools lightly. That, coupled with his name and his unusual silvery gray eyes, unnerving in so dark and forbidding a countenance otherwise, had long since earned him the sobriquet Devil. After half an hour exposed to his biting wit, most thought it a fitting one.

"One month, one week, and three days, to be precise," drawled his lordship. "But I am touched that you should have missed me. What have you been up to in my absence?"

"Oh, this and that," returned Mr. Heybridge rather vaguely. "I didn't know you were back until I ran into Lyndhurst yesterday. I came around last night to see you, but Finchley told me you'd gone out. How did you leave your mother?"

"My mother, as usual, is brimming with health and good spirits. I find her almost as fatiguing as I do you. She sends you her love, by the way, and wonders why you continue to put up with me. As for last night"—a faint shudder took him—"I would really prefer to forget it. I dined with Uxbridge, which was a mistake. His brandy was quite undrinkable, I regret to say and his claret only tolerable. Then I allowed myself to be talked into accompanying him to a masked ball at Ranelagh. Really, I can only think I must still have been fatigued from the journey and so not myself."

"Aye, as if you weren't equal to a drive of some fifty miles!" retorted his friend, unimpressed. "Save it for someone who hasn't known you since you were a callow youth, forever coming home with your nose bloodied."

They had started down the stairs together in his lordship's elegant town house, Deveril's hand tucked into his friend's arm. But at that Deveril's unusual eyes took on a faint gleam, and he countered, "As I recall, my nose was not bloodied quite as often as yours was. But if you have forgotten, my dear Charles, I am perfectly willing to refresh your memory."

Charles laughed and flung up one hand in a fencer's gesture. "Never mind. I cry peace! You are too lethal with your fives for me to risk marring my manly beauty, as you put it. Besides, I am far too happy to argue with anyone today," he admitted.

His lordship shot him a cynical glance. "Don't tell me. You are in love again. I should have known it from your disgustingly cheerful demeanor."

"*Again*?" Mr. Heybridge protested indignantly. "Blast you, Dev, you make it sound as if *I'm* the one mamas are forever warning their daughters against. In fact, I'm damned if I know what women see in you. Your manners are execrable, your tailor makes you, as you yourself often point out, and you never make pretty speeches or put yourself out to please anyone. And yet women can't resist you."

"I fear it is my reputation—and my fortune—they can't resist," said his lordship cynically. "I'm a challenge to them. Women never know quite where they stand with me, and like any other rare commodity, my dear Charles, my very indifference spurs them on to try to possess what they cannot have. It is simple human nature."

"Lord, what a complete hand you are," protested Charles, laughing. "Has no one ever turned the tables on you? It would serve you right if they had."

"Depressingly seldom. In fact, a woman with that much imagination might actually stand a chance in captivating me," observed his lordship thoughtfully. "But alas—" Then he broke off, a small smile beginning to play about his lips. "Though now that you mention it, I did meet at least one woman recently who seemed immune to my appeal."

"Aha!" pronounced Mr. Heybridge promptly. "A new charmer! Tell me *all* about her."

His lordship shrugged, half regretting bringing the subject up. "There is very little to tell, except that she seems to have rather more wit than the majority of her sex. I met her last night at Ranelagh, of all places. You would no doubt have found the whole satisfyingly romantic, my dear Charles, for I was actually guilty of rescuing her from an importunate admirer. Really, I must not have been at all myself last night. Such quixotry is more in your line than in mine."

"Oh no you don't! You don't put me off that easily. Who is she?" demanded Charles, highly entertained.

"I regret that in true fairy-tale manner, I never learned her name. We danced in the moonlight and I kissed her, and then we were rudely interrupted by her escort. But not before I managed to recover this." Somewhat mockingly he produced a pale blue kid glove from his breast pocket.

"Good God! Fairy tale indeed!" pronounced Mr. Heybridge, half suspecting his leg was being pulled. "I must confess Devil Deveril in the role of Prince Charming is somewhat hard to swallow. Do you really mean you know nothing more about her?"

"Only that her name is Kit and she first drew my attention by her faint air of mystery—rare indeed, you will admit, among the depressingly eager damsels at Ranelagh Gardens."

"Don't tell me you mean to search all over London for someone who fits that glove? Lord, I'd give a monkey to see that!"

His lordship tucked the glove back into his pocket, unperturbed. "Well, you must admit the hunt has begun to grow devilishly predictable of late," he complained. "At least this presents me with something of a challenge. Though I fear that what I took to be mystery will turn out merely to be dyspepsia in the depressing light of day. She even warned me that masked balls are dangerous."

"Good God, I'd like to meet her," said Mr. Heybridge frankly. "She sounds exactly what you need to put a dent in your colossal vanity."

His lordship shrugged. "But enough of my affairs. Tell me of this new inamorata of yours. Does she possess a harelip or merely a fatal shyness?"

"Damn you, Dev," Mr. Heybridge protested strongly. "I have never fallen in love with anyone with a harelip."

"My mistake," replied his lordship. "That pleasure still awaits you."

"Good God, it's not as bad as that."

"It is precisely as bad as that," pursued his lordship inexorably. "A woman has only to appeal to your protective instincts and you are lost, my dear Charles. Matrons vie with each other to introduce their unmarried daughters to you, the more unpresentable the better. I fear you have a fatal propensity for rescuing the helpless. I lost track when we were youths of the number of abandoned kittens you brought home, or unwanted dogs, only to lose interest in them once they were no longer in need of rescue or some more pitiful object presented itself to your attention."

"Blast you, Dev," Charles protested, torn between laughter and annoyance. "It's not as bad as that! *I'm* not the one called a devil, remember. At any rate, it's nothing like that this time. I tell you, I am in deadly earnest."

His lordship looked unimpressed. "As you were the last half a dozen times, I remember. Do I know her?"

"I don't know. That is, I doubt it. She and her brother came shortly after the new year, and you'd already gone.

Her name is Christina Castleford. She's staying with Lady Danbury.''

The last was said rather defiantly, for Lady Danbury was a matron of notoriously indiscriminate taste. She had been known to endorse any number of persons over the years who later turned out to be less than they seemed.

But after a moment all his lordship said was, ''I see. And the brother? Is he also staying with Lady Danbury?''

''No. He has rooms somewhere, I think. He's an amusing rattle, not very much like his sister. And before you can say anything, I'll admit Christina has very little fortune. Her grandmother does, but that's another story. At any rate, you know I've never been hanging out for a rich wife. Unlike yours, my own fortune is merely modest. I—well, all I can say is that we seem to suit each other in every way. It sounds ridiculous, but I knew almost the first moment I laid eyes on her that she was the one for me.''

His lordship had made no comment during this romantic speech, though he was looking slightly unwell. ''I see,'' he said again. ''Do I take it then that this Miss Castleford felt the same?''

''I should have known you'd make it sound like something out of a vulgar novel,'' said Charles resentfully.

''Then I apologize. But even you must admit this is all rather sudden.'' Then his lordship's brows drew abruptly together, accentuating the saturnine look that had contributed to his sobriquet, and he repeated incredulously, ''Did you say *Castleford*?''

''I know exactly what you're going to say,'' said Charles furiously. ''But I would have thought you were the last person to hold her grandmother's past against her. Anyway, it was all ages ago—long before we were born.''

''My dear Charles,'' his lordship drawled, looking exceedingly unpleasant, ''I thought you said you were done with knight errantry. A harelip would have been mild by comparison. It may have been ages ago, but it's not every young woman who can boast so colorful a grandmother as Barbara Foxcroft. If I remember correctly, she had a series of wealthy protectors before she finally caught the dull eye of our monarch himself. She was at least once legally married, but I believe the paternity of her only daughter has long been shrouded in mystery. I really had no idea you were so ambitious. The granddaughter of a king, even so lackluster a one, is nothing to be sneered at.''

Charles had whitened. "I hate it when you sneer like that,'' he said in a low voice. "It's then I can believe you the devil you're called. Both her grandmother and mother were married respectably, and I don't give a damn who either of them may have slept with. From all I can tell, neither of us can boast much in that department. My father kept any number of mistresses over the years, and yours was almost as notorious as you are. No one cares about that.''

"There is, however, a slight difference.''

"Then perhaps I should make it clear that I have already asked Miss Castleford to do me the honor of becoming my wife, and she has accepted,'' said Charles stiffly.

Instantly his lordship's face shut down, all emotion wiped from it. "Then, naturally I will say no more. Pray accept my felicitations. When may I look forward to meeting the, er, happy bride?''

He had the doubtful felicity of seeing Charles relax slightly. "Thank you. I knew you wouldn't fail me,'' he said gratefully. "As for meeting her, Lady Danbury is giving a small dinner party this evening for—that is—well, in honor of the occasion. I was hoping you would be able to join us.''

"Believe me, I wouldn't miss it for the world,'' pronounced his lordship grimly.

Chapter 3

MISS CHRISTINA CASTLEFORD was still sitting before her dressing table, despite the lateness of the hour, when her brother Robin unceremoniously strolled in without knocking.

"What? Ain't you ready yet?" he demanded in surprise, seeing her staring rather blankly into her mirror, the hare's foot forgotten in her hand. "Lord, if *I* can present myself on time for once in my life, the least you can do is be ready."

Thus caught woolgathering, Miss Castleford jumped and blushed faintly. "You look very nice," she said approvingly, turning to regard her brother critically. "Is that a new rig-out?"

Robin went immediately to view himself in her cheval glass, well pleased with his appearance. He was an attractive youth, dressed in the requisite long-tailed coat and knee breeches which became him admirably. His chestnut locks were carefully brushed, his shirt points were fashionably high, and he looked, as he would have said himself, a very Go among the Go's.

"Delivered just this morning," he admitted, adjusting the set across his shoulders. "My tailor, curse his mercenary soul, had the damned cheek to dun me for that last coat he made for me, so there was nothing for it but to order another one from him straightaway. But I must admit I'm pleased enough with it.''

Miss Castleford accepted this novel piece of financing without a blink, for she knew her brother well. She did ask, apparently without much hope of being attended to, ''And what happens when the bill comes due?''

''God knows,'' Robin answered cheerfully, going to sprawl on her bed. ''I certainly don't. Perhaps I'll be dead by then. Or the tailor will, plague take him. Or I may have such a run of luck at the faro table that all my problems will be solved. You never know.''

''Why is it that one only hears of someone losing a fortune at the tables?'' inquired his sister judiciously. ''And, if it comes to that, what became of the money you got last night, which cost me so dismal an evening?''

Robin shrugged. ''Good Lord, what ever happens to money? I had to pay some of it on account for my lodgings—rascally landlord was threatening to chuck me out, damn his eyes—and then I met a fellow with a sure tip at Newmarket. One thing led to another and somehow most of it's gone. You know how it is.''

She sighed, for she did indeed know exactly how it was. ''I sometimes think we have no head for money at all,'' she said gloomily. ''I had determined to remain beforehand with the world, but everything has been so very much more expensive in London than I anticipated, and now I have my bride clothes to think of as well.'' She shook her head, as if trying to discover where all the money had gone.

''It's in the blood, my girl,'' Robin said flippantly. ''Better swallow your pride and apply to our notorious grandmama. She's disgustingly full of juice, God knows.''

''I don't think Grandmama is going to be inclined to advance me any money at the moment,'' pointed out Christina rather dryly.

Robin grinned. "Aye, well, order your bride clothes on tick and present the bills to Charles after you're married, then," he suggested with cheerful insouciance. "After all, you will merely be anticipating events slightly."

She didn't even bother to grace that with an answer. "Just don't, I beg of you, try to borrow money from Charles yourself," she said urgently. "At least until he has had a chance to get used to us. He doesn't understand the kind of life we lead, and might find our . . . method of living somewhat unusual."

"Lord, then he's no business marrying into this family," Robin said bluntly. "At any rate, he's unlikely to find it preferable to have his future brother-in-law clapped into debtor's prison."

"Well, I can let you have a hundred or so, if you're badly dipped," she said resignedly. "But it will have to do until after the wedding."

"Bless you." Robin had picked up a silk fan lying on her bed and now spread it open, wholly unconcerned. "Very pretty," he pronounced. "A gift from Charles?"

"Yes." Something in his voice made her put the hare's foot down again and turn to face him, choosing her words with care. "Robin, I know you don't understand, but this is important to me. You may not like Charles, but—"

"Don't worry. I've no wish to endanger the match, m'dear," Robin interrupted in amusement. "In fact, I shall find it convenient to have so eminently respectable a brother-in-law." He darted a look up at her from between his lashes and added in a murmur, "Though at the risk of sounding vain, I think you could have done very much better for yourself. However much we may resent her, you are Barbara Foxcroft's granddaughter after all, and *she* was accounted a dazzling beauty. Your precious Charles's fortune is only moderate and I suspect his earnest respectability will begin to pall all too soon.''

''Don't sneer!'' she flared unexpectedly. ''Good God, you make respectability sound like a curse.''

''Well, isn't it? Certainly we've precious little in our family to boast of.'' He spread the fan again and asked idly, ''Why'd you do it? Betroth yourself to the worthy Charles, I mean. I've often wondered. You might have had your pick of far more eligible *partis*, you know.''

She struggled uselessly with how to make him understand. ''If you must know, I think it's the respectability that most appealed to me,'' she offered unwillingly after a long moment. ''You've seen what it's like, Robin. The snubs and disapproving looks and even the improper offers, all because I'm Barbara Foxcroft's granddaughter. Charles was different, and I think I'll always be grateful to him, if only for that. As for the money, it has never mattered so much to me, though it will be wonderful to live without the specter of bailiffs forever at the door and always having to pinch and scrape and count pennies. Oh, what's the use? You will only sneer. But to be Mrs. Charles Heybridge and have a home and family and security—all the things we've never had— seems like heaven to me. Can you understand that, even a little?''

''Lord, m'dear, better you than me,'' Robin said frankly. ''It all sounds devilish boring to me. But if that's how you feel, my advice to you is to marry your dull Charles quickly, before he has second thoughts or Grandmama gets wind of it. I fear she lacks your love of respectability, and will consider him but a poor enough bargain. You know she had ambitions of your emulating her own success at the very least.''

''Yes, but I doubt even Grandmama would wish me to

follow exactly in her footsteps,'' retorted Christina a little tartly.

''I wouldn't be too sure,'' Robin said with a grin. ''Face it, m'dear, we're hardly a conventional family. I only hope dear Charles knows what he's getting into.''

Because she herself in her weaker moments wondered the same, Christina's voice was unnecessarily sharp: ''We should go down. Charles may have arrived already, and he is bringing a friend with him. I don't want to be late.''

Robin obediently pulled himself off the bed and straightened his coat. ''Only take care, m'dear, that all this dull domesticity don't begin to pall on you after a very little while. You can't be that different from me.''

Christina ignored that and led the way downstairs, trying to still the unaccustomed butterflies in her stomach over the coming evening. She should have known that despite the closeness between them Robin would understand little of what she was talking about. He seemed genuinely not to care that he lived constantly on the brink of ruin. He would blithely ignore the mounting duns until the tipstaffs were at the door, then borrow off his friends or, if no other alternative offered itself, post back to Foxcroft, where he would eat crow for a space of time until he had managed to wheedle just enough out of their disapproving grandmother to stave off disaster for another six months. Then the whole would begin over again.

It was an exhausting life, as Christina well knew from bitter experience. Their mama had been just such another, irresponsible and extravagant, with never a notion where the money went or any idea of economy. Their childhood had been rendered hideous by the continuous presence of duns and bailiffs and the resulting hysterical scenes they induced.

In the end their mama would be forced to reconcile with their disapproving grandmama, with whom she had quarreled years before. Barbara Foxcroft would exact her pound of flesh before reluctantly bailing them out yet again, but invariably, once the worst of the bills had been settled, Mrs. Castleford would embark on a new round of extravagance, eternally convinced that next time things would be different.

They never were, of course, and Christina could little blame their grandmother when she finally washed her hands of them. Her papa, a colorless middle-class individual whom Christina could scarcely remember and whose only rash act seemed to have been to marry their mama in the teeth of his rigidly upright family's horror, had had the good sense to die long since, no doubt exhausted by the turmoil and his wife's extravagance.

Their mother had herself died some three years ago, worn out by a life of living constantly on the brink of ruin. Barbara Foxcroft had once more reluctantly stepped in, paying off her daughter's debts one last time and taking possession of her grandchildren.

Afterward Christina was to think of it in exactly that way, for it quickly became apparent that Barbara Foxcroft had not lost any of her old ambition. Having been bitterly failed by her only daughter, she clearly saw her handsome grandchildren as her last chance to achieve the social acceptance that had so long eluded her. She might have made a fortune from her youthful indiscretions, and invested it wisely so that she was now a very wealthy woman, but she had remained a social outcast, shunned by the scandalously disapproving majority.

In her beautiful granddaughter she hoped to correct that. If she had achieved a king, she saw no reason why Christina should not do almost as well, parlaying her youth and beauty into an advantageous—and this time legal—alliance. Unfortunately in her book charm and likeability took a distant

second place to wealth and title, and on that scale Charles
was not at all likely to impress her.

It was she who had financed this one London Season,
determined to make it pay off. Christina would herself have
preferred one of the watering places, for she had had a
lifetime in which to learn that her grandmother's notoriety
was far from forgotten by a disapproving world. To a ten-
year-old faced with the reality of a schoolmate who couldn't
come to visit because her grandmother had once been the
mistress of the king, it had seemed very unfair. But she had
enough worldliness now to know that there was a great deal
in life that wasn't fair.

But Grandmama had insisted upon London and had
arranged for an old acquaintance, Lady Danbury, to
chaperone her. Vouchers for Almack's were clearly beyond
them, but she had hopes that her granddaughter's undeniable
beauty, coupled with Lady Danbury's support, would open
a great many doors to them.

Well, some doors had indeed been opened. But a great
many more had been closed, and a number of shoulders
coldly turned to her. Christina, facing the daily snubs and
insinuations and outright rudeness, had hated every minute
of it, and only her pride, and the knowledge that there was
no future for her back at Foxcroft either, had kept her from
giving up and running back to lick her wounds in private.

It was then that, almost miraculously, Charles Heybridge
had come into her life. He had witnessed a painful snub
delivered to her at a ball one evening by a stiff-backed
dowager, and promptly asked her to dance. He was
charming, kind, everything Christina had begun to think she
dared not hope for, and when he had asked for her hand less
than a fortnight after they met, she had accepted him with
grateful affection.

Even more miraculously, he seemed genuinely not to care

a fig for her grandmother's reputation. Both his parents were dead, which under the circumstances must prove a plus, and he possessed only one sister, much younger than himself, who was at present away on an extended visit to friends in the north.

In short, he was almost too good to be true. He was kind and understanding, gentle and protective, with considerable personal charm and appealing warmth, but his family was by no means remarkable and his fortune merely respectable. He had no desire to gain a reputation among the *ton* or make himself ridiculous by the exaggeration of his clothes or the dryness of his wit, all of which Christina despised. If he had not exactly swept her off her feet, and she liked and respected rather than loved him, she was practical enough to think that was perhaps just as well. Love would surely follow, and she knew far too much of her family's fatal history to have much faith in one's emotions.

If the memory of a highly romantic encounter indeed and a stolen kiss in the moonlight from the devil himself annoyingly insisted upon intruding, somehow making a mockery of such sober declarations, she was mostly able to thrust it back into her subconscious where it belonged.

At any rate, she had more than enough to occupy her at the moment. There were only two fears to mar her present happiness, both of them unpleasantly nagging. The first was that in her weaker moments, she could not quite dismiss the suspicion that in accepting Charles's offer she was condemning him to more than he knew. She told herself that he was a grown man who surely must know his own mind, and she had disguised nothing of her past. But to know something and to live it were unfortunately two different things.

The second fear was his friends and relations. However much Charles might be willing to disregard her notorious grandmother, his sister and his best friend were unlikely to be so forgiving.

It made the coming evening more of an ordeal than she liked, for she could not help but feel as if she were on trial. Charles had laughed at her and assured her that Deveril could not help but like her. But she had already discovered that Charles, like Robin, tended to ignore problems, thinking they would go away. She envied him that insouciance but lacked his optimism.

The guests had already arrived as she and Robin went downstairs, for she could hear voices coming from the drawing room. She told herself that Deveril could not fault her appearance at least, for she knew without vanity that she and Robin together made a striking couple. Robin was in his new blue coat, and whatever his failings, he seldom failed to turn heads when he passed. And she had chosen for the occasion a simple gown of jonquil gauze that flattered her difficult coloring.

But it was still with a distinct sense of trepidation that she entered the drawing room. Lady Danbury was the first to see them and beamed upon them with some pride. She was a cheerful widow of stout proportions whose reduced circumstances had induced her to undertake the chaperonage of such a controversial guest. Christina happened to know that her grandmother was paying her an outrageous fee, but it seemed at least to have bought her goodwill, for she pretended not to see the many snubs they received and had behaved toward Christina throughout with unexpected tolerance.

Unfortunately, she had less than common sense and frequently irritated Christina with her foolish prattle. But she said happily now, "Oh, here you both are. I swear, I never cease to marvel at the resemblance between you. It's like looking at two peas in a pod. And both so handsome! Don't you think so, Mr. Heybridge? But of course," she added archly, "I should know your opinion by now."

Charles laughed and rose to greet his betrothed. "I do, but perhaps I'm a little prejudiced," he agreed, smiling down into Christina's eyes and lightly kissing her hand. "We shall have to get Blaise Deveril's opinion on the matter. He is a noted connoisseur, you know."

The fifth member of the party had been seated out of Christina's sight. He rose now, however, and Christina saw him for the first time.

For a moment her blood froze, and she could not quite grasp the enormity of the jest that fate had played on her. For Charles's best friend to be the man she had danced with and kissed in the moonlight the night before seemed the height of cruel mischance.

Then Deveril advanced upon her, unmistakeable anger and contempt in his cold silver eyes, and drawled unpleasantly, "An intriguing sight indeed. You didn't tell me, Charles, that Miss Castleford and her brother were twins."

Chapter 4

IT WAS LIKE a nightmare. Christina's brief and inexplicable behavior of the night before had come back to haunt her many times in the past twenty-four hours, for it was unlike her to be swept off her feet by a handsome and mysterious stranger. Certainly she had never in a million years expected to meet him again so soon and under such unbelievable circumstances.

She had gone with Robin last night only at his insistence, and after her unpleasant evening she had informed him on the way home that she would not be so accommodating again. She had had an unpleasant hour or so while Robin had disappeared on his own business, and the mysterious stranger in the black domino had by no means been the worst of the cavaliers who had accosted her.

But then, an unwelcome voice reminded her, she had not waltzed with them in the moonlight, or lost her head completely as the result of a few dizzying kisses. Nor had she wasted more than a few moments in the long night watches in remembering them, as she had in dreaming of a tall, romantic stranger come to sweep her off her feet.

Aye, but that was the stuff that fairy tales were made of, and reality had long ago taught her that such dreams had little to do with her life. In the cold light of day she could hardly explain what had led her to behave so uncharacteristically. In general, no doubt because of the ever present reminder of her grandmother, she tended to be undemonstrative and even straitlaced. Not for her the casual kisses and daring flirtations she had seen going on all around her last night. She was too afraid of being tarred with her grandmother's reputation not to keep her feet firmly on the ground.

It was doubly ironic, then, that her first lapse should have been with the best friend of the man she was betrothed to. She had no idea what Deveril would do. Denounce her immediately? Drawl in that unpleasant voice, "Why yes, Miss Castleford and I met last night, when I rescued her from one drunken fool and made improper advances to her myself?"

And if he did, what would she—could she—say in her defense? That for the first time in her life she had been swept beyond her cool caution and had already come to regret it? That that brief taste of passion had been as frightening as it was exhilarating, and that she had aleady learned her lesson?

But it seemed Deveril did not mean to expose her, at least for the moment. Instead he advanced on her with his hand held out and that same contempt deep in his eyes. "How do you do, Miss Castleford? I must congratulate you on the success of your entrance. Apart, you and your brother must always be remarkable because of your coloring. But together you are magnificent. But then you probably know that already."

It was said unpleasantly, as all the rest had been. So, he might not mean to renounce her for the moment, but he didn't mean for her to go unpunished. Still, she had no choice but to try to brazen it out. She reluctantly took the hand he offered and said cooly, "How do you do, my lord? I have heard a great deal about you from Charles."

His brows rose, and he did not immediately release her hand, though she tried instantly to withdraw it. "Have you, Miss Castleford?" he inquired. "I fear for my part you have come as a . . . complete surprise."

Miraculously Charles did not notice anything wrong, for he protested laughingly, "Not an unpleasant one, I hope? At any rate, don't try to pretend I didn't bend your ear the whole way here singing her praises."

She dared to raise her eyes to Deveril's mocking glance. "That must have been boring for your lordship."

"On the contrary. I found it most intriguing. He told me, for instance, Miss Castleford, that you were an angel. But with that hair I would beg leave to doubt it. Are you an angel, Miss Castleford?"

She flushed, as he had known she would. Still, she would not give him the satisfaction of knowing she was afraid of him. "Far from it, my lord," she answered indifferently. "Is anyone?" She turned away to carelessly adjust the train of her dress, praying no one would notice her heightened color or the fury in her eyes.

Charles laughed. "He should talk. You must know, my dear, that he is called Devil by most of those who know him."

"Is that so, my lord?" she inquired politely. "And are you? A devil, I mean?"

She thought she saw reluctant admiration in his eyes, but he countered readily, "I believe some have reason to think so. But you must admit it is an odd combination. The devil and an angel in the same room. Though I somehow doubt that either of us wholly lives up to our reputation, do we, Miss Castleford?"

She should have known better than to fence with him. She flushed even more deeply, but luckily Charles intervened: "Enough, enough. This is turning into a ridiculous conversation. Allow me to present instead Mr. Robert Castleford, Christina's brother.''

"And I am certainly no angel," said Robin with a grin, shaking his lordship's hand. But there was a curious speculation in his deep blue eyes, so like her own.

After that Deveril seemed to choose to withdraw his sword, at least for the moment, for the conversation turned to other topics and Christina was able to breathe again.

But she dared not relax. The next hours passed in somewhat of a fog, for she never dared quite lower her guard under that mocking glance. Every time she looked up, it was to find his unpleasant silver eyes on her, and by the end of the evening she was ready to swear that he was in truth the devil he was called.

Luckily, no one else seemed to guess that anything was amiss, for Lady Danbury was sparkling, flattered to have such a distinguished guest, Charles was his usual cheerful self, and Lord Deveril himself now smoothly polite. Only Robin, looking between them curiously now and again, seemed to suspect anything, and if so he was thankfully keeping his conclusions to himself.

Only once during the course of that interminable evening did Christina find herself alone with Deveril. The gentlemen had not lingered over their port, instead rejoining the ladies almost at once, and Charles and Robin were lightly discussing something while Lady Danbury occupied herself with her embroidery. She complained of a chill, since the evening had turned damp, and Christina, grateful for any excuse to escape even for a moment, willingly rose to fetch a shawl for her.

She lingered upstairs on her errand as long as she dared, dreading to return to the drawing room and those mocking silver eyes. She did not know what Deveril intended, but she had little hope that she had heard the end of the affair.

Last night he had said he would find her again, but she had believed it merely an idle promise prompted by the moonlight and the moment. And neither of them could have predicted the circumstances of their next meeting.

Well, if he had indeed been infatuated with her last night, it seemed clear the emotion had not lasted beyond being introduced to her as his best friend's fiancée. Now he clearly despised her, and she could not hope he would long keep that emotion to himself. Her hopes seemed to her to be in the dust, for even supposing Deveril remained silent and she married Charles, he would always be there in the background with his unpleasant sneer, threatening her happiness and peace of mind.

It was thus with a heavy heart she at last reluctantly made her way back downstairs, only to find Lord Deveril in the hall waiting for her.

She checked, feeling an uncomfortable frisson of fear down her spine. Then she made herself straighten and continue on down the last few stairs. He could not murder her, after all, though he might look as if the prospect were a pleasant one to him, and if she had learned anything it was to confront unpleasantness with one's head high and no hint of being touched by it.

"Are you leaving, Lord Deveril?" she inquired calmly, keeping a pleasant expression on her face, though it almost killed her to do so.

He smiled rather wolfishly and took Lady Danbury's shawl from her. "I'm sorry to disappoint you," he said mockingly, "but Lady Danbury was merely wondering what had become of you, so I volunteered to come and look for you."

Christina had never regretted Lady Danbury's placid blindness more. "Then I'd better not delay any longer," she said lightly, and made to pass him.

At once he deliberately barred her way. "Not so quickly, Red."

Her eyes again flashed up to his at the hated nickname, their fury undisguised this time. "Don't call me that! I despise that nickname."

He merely laughed. "I think you would prefer it to some other names I might call you. But it seems you vastly underrate your charms, my dear. You warned me, as I recall, that were we to meet under ordinary circumstances I would find you hopelessly commonplace. The granddaughter of Barbara Foxcroft may be many things, but I could not consider commonplace among them."

She flushed under his insults but raised her chin and demanded bluntly, "Why didn't you tell Charles about last night?"

He shrugged his broad shoulders, very much at his ease. "Why didn't you, if it comes to that? Or need I ask? I would be curious to know who your cavalier was last night, by the way. Certainly it wasn't Charles."

Pride prevented her from admitting it had been Robin, for she discovered she would prefer almost anything than to appear to crawl before this man. She doubted he would believe her anyway. It was obvious he had made up his mind about her and had no intention of listening to reason.

Watching her closely, he smiled again at her continued silence. "Cat got your tongue, eh, Red? I can't say that I blame you. It might be somewhat difficult to explain that you were deceiving both of them by kissing me in the moonlight. It would seem you mean to outdo even the notoriety your grandmother achieved."

Every word was an insult, and she had to ball her fists to keep from striking the sneer from that hateful face. She could not imagine now how she had ever found him intriguing. "Then tell Charles!" she snapped, and made once more to pass him.

Again he barred her, very sure of himself and his hold over her. "Oh, no! I fear it's not quite that easy, Red."

His hand on her arm seemed to burn her and she glared down at it. He laughed and removed it, reminding her insultingly, "You didn't despise my touch last night, as I recall."

"You—I—" She knew it was hopeless, but she couldn't give up her dream so easily, couldn't help trying to make him understand. "Last night was . . . a temporary aberration," she said helplessly. "A moon madness, as you yourself said. It meant nothing and it will certainly not happen again."

"Do you think so? You disappoint me, Red," he said softly, hatefully.

"Oh, you *devil*," she whispered, as if against her will.

Again he laughed. "I thought we had already established that fact. And you, you beautiful, faithless jade, far from being the angel my poor deluded friend thinks, are a fit consort for me. But Charles doesn't know that, does he? Yet."

She would have walked away then, threat or no threat, had he not held her with a hard grip and added unsmilingly, "But we can't talk here. We are likely to have been missed already. Meet me in the park tomorrow morning at eight. And don't even think of failing me, for I will come here and drag you out if I have to. And I don't think you want that."

Before she could wrest her arm from his long fingers, he had politely opened the door for her. She had no option but to hold her head high and precede him into the room, praying no one would guess how rapidly her heart pounded in her breast or her eyes burned with unshed tears of self-pity and fury.

It was late when she was at last able to retire to her room, and she was so drained she could scarcely hold her head up. The rest of the evening had passed off somehow, though she had little recollection of it, nor did she have any idea what she meant to do. The only thing she knew for a certainty was that the idea of being in Deveril's power was enough to make her grind her teeth with impotent rage.

She was worldly enough to know that if he had refrained from telling Charles about her it was for his own ends, not out of any innate chivalry. Nor did blackmail seem by any means out of character for him.

Well, if he tried blackmail, she had little doubt what form that blackmail would take. She would give Charles up and disappear before that, of course, if for no other reason than she thought she would die first before putting herself any further in that devil's hands.

If Deveril offered her a slip on the shoulder she might, of course, use that against him with Charles. But the thought was a depressing one, conjuring up visions of endless unpleasantness. She thought she would indeed prefer to disappear first, for she had sufficient conceit not to wish to bring turmoil and unhappiness with her along with her bride clothes.

Oh, damn Deveril, she thought. At the moment she could see no way out of his vise, and could only rely upon the morning to bring her fresher counsel. If not, she was in danger of seeing all her own and her grandmama's ambitions defeated by a trick of malign fate.

On that dismal thought she began to undress, but was soon interrupted by a scratching on her door. She feared it was Lady Danbury come for a late-night chat, and was tempted to pretend to be already asleep. But it was Robin's voice that said softly through the panels, "Open up, Kit. I know you're not asleep yet, and I want to talk to you."

Resignedly she pulled on her wrapper and went to open the door for him. "Go away, Robin," she begged him wearily. "I am not fit company for anyone at the moment."

He merely grinned and lounged in. "So I wasn't mistaken there was something going on tonight? Tell Uncle Robin all about it."

She was in no mood for his sometimes inappropriate sense of humor, but knew her brother well enough to know he wouldn't rest until he had dragged the truth from her. At any rate, he was her twin. He might be careless and impudent, but because of that strong tie between them they were closer than most brothers and sisters, and had been in the habit of telling each other everything.

So she poured out to him the whole miserable tale of the night before and its unpleasant consequences.

He whistled, but she could tell by the look in his eyes that he was a little amused as well. "Whew! Did you really let him kiss you?" he asked curiously.

"It was scarcely a question of *let*," she insisted somewhat untruthfully. "And if you hadn't dragged me there in the first place, none of this would have happened."

"Aye, but then I warned you you were likely to find all this dull domesticity beginning to pall sooner or later," Robin pointed out with annoying complacency.

She had seldom found herself less in charity with him. "If that is the only advice you have to give, then I wish you would go away and let me get some sleep," she answered sharply, climbing into bed.

"Oh, I've more advice for you, but I doubt you're likely to find it any more palatable. It was obvious to me, if not that dull fiancé of yours, that Deveril couldn't take his eyes off you at dinner tonight."

"Only because he despises me."

"Well, you might call it that, though I have another name

for it," he grinned. "But you must admit he's a far better catch than Charles. Don't eat me! I'm just pointing out that you could do worse if he fancies you. There's the title, and I understand he has a considerable fortune. Whatever you may think of him, you must admit he's an intriguing devil. I fear he makes poor Charles look bloodless by comparison."

She almost shuddered. "Don't say that, even in jest. I think I would rather die first. Anyway, if he wants me, it won't be marriage he's offering, you can be sure of that."

Robin shrugged. "Ah, well. Then it seems you have no other choice than to marry the dull Charles out of hand. You can fob him off with some tale or another, and by the time Deveril can expose you it will be too late."

Christina flushed and for some reason could not quite meet her brother's eyes. "Thank you, but if Charles is at all likely to change his mind, I would far prefer him to know it before rather than after the wedding."

Robin rose and yawned. "You've far too many scruples, m'dear," he said frankly. "In that case, if you won't trick Charles into an immediate marriage and you've no fancy to become Deveril's mistress, it seems you've only one other choice. Tell Charles the truth. At the moment he's probably even besotted enough to believe you."

He halted at the door. "But don't forget that I warned you about trying to make yourself into something you aren't. We're not respectable like other people, m'dear. And marrying Charles isn't likely to change that. Now I'm off to bed. All in all, it was a dull evening and I can't keep my eyes open."

Christina determinedly closed her ears to his prophetic words and blew out her candle, only wishing she could close her mind as easily.

Chapter 5

CHRISTINA SLEPT BADLY that night and rose with a heavy heart, still undecided whether to meet Deveril or not. On the one hand, she desired nothing so much as to teach him she was not at his beck and call. But on the other, she was not certain she dared call his bluff and risk having him come to Lady Danbury's to see her.

In the end it seemed easier to do as he suggested—at least this one time. She therefore dressed and let herself out of the still sleeping house, grateful for the indifference of London-trained housemaids, who merely looked at her curiously before returning to their dusting.

Still more fortunately, she met few people out and about so early, and no one she knew. One or two horsemen ogled her rather pointedly as they passed, and the Household Cavalry, out for their morning exercises, rode smartly past, but it was still far too early for the myriad walkers and riders and carriages that would clog Hyde Park later that day during the fashionable promenade.

It was also still too early for there to be any real warmth in the day, and she huddled into her light pelisse. But she suspected that the chill she felt had more to do with her errand than the cool morning air.

When she reached the appointed rendezvous, it was to find Lord Deveril there before her. Having dismounted, he held the reins of a handsome black and was looking around him rather impatiently.

When he saw her the brief satisfaction on his harsh face made her long to smack it. "So, you came," he observed, not even bothering to show any triumph. He took in her stylish walking dress of bottle green, and at least she had the satisfaction of seeing a reluctant admiration come into his eyes. "You look very expensive," he added offensively. "Did Charles's money pay for that?"

She made herself ignore that transparent provocation. "I came for the first and last time," she answered coldly. "Say what you have to say and get it over."

He was merely amused. "Oh, I think you know well enough what I have to say, Miss Castleford, but I doubt you will find any of it to your liking. You have been exceedingly clever but not quite clever enough, I fear."

"Are you always this quick to judge others?" she demanded bitterly. "You know nothing of me, Lord Deveril. Nothing."

"On the contrary, I know everything I need. To learn that you are Barbara Foxcroft's granddaughter is enough. You are every bit as beautiful as she was reputed to be, and have undoubtedly also inherited her capacity for deceit. And don't bother flashing those magnificent eyes of yours at me," he added mockingly. "You do it very well, and it's undoubtedly becoming, but I regret I lack Charles's susceptibility. And don't forget that I know that within a few days or weeks of your betrothal to him, you were kissing me. Hardly the behavior of a modest and virtuous woman, I think you will agree?"

"*I* was kissing *you*? Why, you—you—"

"Devil?" he asked in amusement. "No, I know exactly

who you are, Miss Castleford. But I bear you no particular ill will. Remove your claws from Charles and I promise I will become your greatest admirer."

So, it had come. She said disdainfully, "If I am unmoved by your dislike, my lord, I am unlikely to be moved by your favor."

He merely shrugged. "You could do worse. Charles is unworthy of your mettle, Red."

"I told you not to call me that!" Then she was sorry to have given him so much satisfaction, for he looked amused. "And you *are* worthy of my mettle, I suppose, Lord Deveril?" She put all of her contempt into the words.

But he seemed supremely untouched by it. "Or failing me, some other. Perhaps in your shoes you are wise to insist upon marriage. After all, you have your grandmother's lesson before you. As I said, I have no objection to that, providing Charles is not your groom. But you may find marriage less amenable than you think it. After all, it does require some semblance of fidelity, or at least the appearance of it. If you should ever change your mind and contemplate a more . . . elastic arrangement, you will find me, er, your willing slave."

"Your effrontery is only exceeded by your incredible vanity, my lord."

"I don't see why. We have already proven our compatibility. And you will not find me ungenerous. I will set you up in the style to which you would like to become accustomed, and give you almost as much security as marriage with none of the disadvantages. I am also unlikely to enact jealous scenes, as poor Charles will, or care overmuch what you do out of my company. Think it over, Red. You might find that, like your grandmother, you prefer the freedom of such an arrangement to the more inflexible demands of the wedding ring."

It was no more than she had expected, but she found the reality more degrading even than she had imagined. "And I suppose if I don't agree, you will tell Charles of our first meeting?" she demanded in contempt.

He actually laughed. "You overestimate yourself, Red. I believe I am unlikely to put myself to so much trouble for any woman. Nor have I any desire to blackmail you into my bed. We both know I don't need to."

She almost ground her teeth. "It is you who overestimate yourself, my lord. Having kept silent last night, you may find you have overplayed your hand this time."

He grinned appreciatively. "So, you are a gambler along with everything else, are you? I should have suspected as much. In that case, I will offer you excellent odds on the likelihood of your ever bringing Charles Heybridge to church. The day you succeed in doing so, I will pay you five thousand pounds with no strings attached. I will even put it in writing if you wish."

"Thinking, no doubt, that you hold all the cards? Well, my lord, you may find the deck has not been wholly dealt out yet. Are you so sure Charles will even believe you? After all, I have no doubt you have made little secret of the fact you disapprove of me." She saw the sudden, betraying flicker of his eyes and was satisfied. "He may merely believe this yet another attempt to discredit me."

"I said last night you were clever." His tone betrayed little but genuine admiration. "But are you so willing to put it to the test? It seems to me you have far more to lose than I have."

She thought she hated him more than she had ever hated any other human being, but she would not give him the satisfaction of seeing it in her face. "What makes you so certain I haven't told Charles already?"

But that didn't even slow him. "Because, my dear," he

said confidently, "you would not have met me this morning if you had. And because you are far too clever to do anything until you had made sure of exactly how much of a threat I was likely to prove."

"Again you overestimate yourself, my lord. You will never prove a threat to me."

He merely smiled. "I think we both know that is not true, Red. But you may relax. I have no intention of telling Charles about the other night."

She gaped at him, not quite certain she had heard him right and far from believing she could trust him. "You haven't—? Do you seriously expect me to believe that?"

"You may believe it or not." He shrugged. "It happens to be the truth."

It took her a moment to gather her wits. "Why have you told me that?" she asked slowly. "If you indeed mean it, then you must know you have lost whatever hold you might ever have had over me. And you are not precisely known for your philanthropy, I believe."

"But nor am I a fool, Miss Castleford. You are quite right. Were I to inform Charles of our little moonlight escapade the other night, he might be sufficiently disgusted to wash his hands of you. But the odds are as great that he would merely blame me and put an end to our friendship. You see I am being admirably frank with you. I don't say that loss would cause me an unhealable wound, but I have few enough friends that I value those I possess."

"But if you know that, why have you dared to say the things you have said to me?" she demanded incredulously.

"Nothing has changed between us, Red. You still will not wed Charles Heybridge," he asserted with annoying confidence. "But I have every intention that the coming battle shall be between us alone."

"But this is incredible! I begin to think you are mad, not

merely overimpressed with your own importance. You have said you will not use the one weapon you have against me, and yet you still expect me to meekly give up my plans to marry Charles?''

''You might call it enlightened self-interest. I have said I would not use that threat against you. I haven't said I had no others.''

''What others?'' she demanded scoffingly.

He smiled, and for some reason she felt a small tremor run down her spine. ''Ah, you do right to tremble, Miss Castleford,'' he said with satisfaction. ''I am, after all, the devil. I might have you kidnapped until your fascination for Charles had worn off—which believe me, it will. I might even arrange to have you disappear permanently. I will confess the thought of that has given me some pleasant moments.''

''Oh, this is ridiculous, my lord,'' she cried. ''You talk in terms more suited to the stage than real life.''

''Try me and see.''

She could not believe he was serious. He might look like the devil, but he would not dare try so drastic a remedy in this day and age. Did he really believe they were still living in some desperate times, when such threats might really have had some weight with her? Or that there would be no one to prevent him? ''I fear you have started to take your own reputation far too seriously, my lord. The truth is, were I to wed Charles tomorrow, there is nothing you could do about it, and we both know it.''

He merely shrugged. ''I can only repeat, try it and see.''

As if to convince herself as much as him, she added vehemently, ''Oh, these vague threats get us nowhere. In point of fact, you are powerless and you know it. Charles is fully of age, and I have never made any secret of my grandmother's past.''

"Yes, you have admittedly been very clever, but not quite clever enough. You should have had the ring on your finger before I returned. Failing that, you would do better to count your losses and find some other victim. I promise I will put no obstacle in your way to marriage with anyone else, providing you can achieve it. I will even wish you every success."

"Your generosity is overwhelming."

She might have known he would be as untouched by her sarcasm as by everything else. He added softly, "But you will not wed Charles, and that you may count on, Red."

It was like talking to a brick wall. "Even assuming you were right and I had somehow tricked Charles into marriage, why should it matter to you?" she demanded in frustration. "You are not his keeper. Nor, I must say, have you the reputation of caring what happens to anyone but yourself."

"Oh, I'll admit that when Charles first told me he was planning to wed the granddaughter of Barbara Foxcroft, I was appalled, but had no intention of doing anything to prevent it," he admitted indifferently.

"Then why? One would almost think that you were jealous, which is ridiculous. You plainly have no heart."

"You may say I discovered in myself a constitutional dislike of seeing such a predatory harpy as you take advantage of so good a man as Charles. Does that surprise you? I may lack Charles's goodness, but I am still capable of recognizing it in others, I believe."

She held back her fury with an effort and said stiffly, dismissingly, "Then if you are convinced I am such an unworthy wife for Charles, tell him so by all means and see how far it gets you. And if you don't dare, spare me any more of your toothless threats."

"Oh, you shall soon learn whether my threats are toothless or not, Miss Castleford. In fact, I give you fair warning, since I consider myself a sporting man. If you do not relish a fight with me—and you would be well advised not to—then withdraw your claws from Charles and find another victim. I will undertake not to impede you in that search and even wish you well. If not, then proceed at your own risk, for I will allow neither your sex nor your undoubted beauty to weigh with me. That is just a friendly warning, by the way.''

"You—you—oh, I knew it was a waste of time trying to talk to you. You are very generous with your threats, my lord. Now hear mine! If you value your friendship with Charles—and despite everything, oddly enough I think you do—then take care how you alienate me. Were I, for instance, to tell Charles of that night, but in my own terms, I think it would be you, not me, who would suffer the most. And though I wouldn't like to cause a rift between you, if you care to see Charles after we are wed, you had best take care to remain on good terms with me. Do I make myself clear?''

"Oh, perfectly, Miss Castleford," he drawled. "And you would be advised to remember my threats as well, for I meant every word. You will not marry Charles Heybridge.''

When she remained furiously silent, he added softly, "What's more, I suspect I shall infinitely enjoy the coming fight, though I doubt you will be able to say the same, Red. Shall we shake hands on our pact? But then, that would be the civilized thing to do, and we are neither of us, under the skin, particularly civilized, are we, sweetheart?''

She turned without another word and strode away, afraid to trust herself any longer.

Despite his insults, she told herself, he had played right into her hands. Were she to tell Charles that he had made her an indecent proposal, it would gut much of Deveril's protests about her. In fact, it would serve him right, for the

chances were high that Charles would indeed end his friendship with him there and then.

But even as the thought formed, she realized she had no
intention of telling Charles about her dealings with Deveril.
Perhaps it was as inexplicable as his refusal to use his one
sure weapon against her, but she had no wish for Charles
to know all the humiliating details. At any rate Deveril was
right about one thing at least. The coming battle was between
them alone. And for all his threats he would soon learn she
was not so easily intimidated.

Even so, there had been much about the recent hateful
meeting that puzzled and disturbed her. Deveril's wild threats
she easily dismissed, considering them no more than an
attempt to frighten her. But his reluctance to involve Charles
was more perplexing. He must know that with one blow he
could easily undermine Charles's faith in her. And yet he
chose not to deliver that blow.

It was also plain he still desired her, but he had chosen
as well not to hold his threats over her head to force her
capitulation—at least so far. He would not have succeeded,
but given what he thought her, he could not have known that.

Probably he was merely so convinced of his own reputation
that he considered his vague threats enough. And if so, he
would soon enough discover his mistake.

But just the same, he was proving a most annoying puzzle,
and one it would do as well not to underestimate.

Chapter 6

In the meantime Lord Deveril, well pleased with the results of his morning's work, strode around to one of his clubs.

He found his uncle dozing before the fire, the morning papers at his elbow and his handkerchief spread over his face.

Deveril ruthlessly poked him. "Wake up, Roddy," he commanded unsympathetically.

The Honorable Roderick Deveril woke with a snort. He was a stout gentleman of a cherubic countenance only slightly overlaid by an air of fashionable world-weariness, and as indolent as he was good-natured. He wore his still dark locks pomaded and curled in the latest fashion, restrained his large person beneath rigid stays that creaked slightly when he bowed or bent over, and, being a product of a more permissive age, happily embellished his person with all manner of rings, chains, fobs, and seals. There was a large gray pearl tucked into the snowy folds of his cravat, and a great emerald stood upon one pudgy forefinger.

By comparison, his nephew seemed almost ascetic. His blue coat recommended itself only by its complete lack of ostentation—and its excellent cut—and no jewelry sullied the pristine plainness of his person. His only affectation was a quizzing glass hung on a string that he could use to deadly effect when confronted by anyone who bored him.

"What the devil—?" demanded Roderick, starting up. Then he recognized his nephew and subsided again, yawning. "Oh, it is the devil, is it?" he added with a certain wry humor. "Heard you was back. How did you leave your mother?"

"Blooming as ever. A month in her company has exhausted me. I had to return to London to get some rest."

"Aye, remarkable woman, your mother," agreed Roderick, stretching out his hand for the glass at his elbow. "Oblige me by pulling that bell, m'boy. You'll take a glass of something? Aye, a fine woman, but too much of a fire eater for my taste. Come to that, you're the same, though. Unrestful," complained his uncle, yawning. "Never know what you're up to."

He eyed his nephew's sardonic expression and added unwillingly, "In fact, you're looking mighty pleased with yourself at the moment. What have you been up to?"

"Slaying a dragon," retorted his lordship promptly, bestirring himself to pull the bell.

"In that case, don't tell me," begged Roddy. "It's bound to exhaust me." He cast a bright, not unintelligent eye up at his nephew and after a moment asked curiously, belying his earlier protestations of indifference, "Did you succeed? In slaying the dragon, I mean."

"Let us say I cast out a lure that should prove successful. Eminently successful," said his lordship, a small smile playing about his mouth.

"Aye, well, better not tell me," protested his uncle again. "That's a devilish fine coat, by the by. Who made it for you? Weston? I swear I've yet to have one from him that fit me half so well. Though anyone who didn't know you would take you for a Quaker in that somber rig," he added disapprovingly.

"Not for long, I trust," said his lordship, at his most saturnine.

"Plague take it, don't trouble to play off those airs with me," grumbled his uncle. "Don't forget I knew you when you was a scrubby brat, all over skinned knees and a dirty face."

His lordship's expression relaxed into something remarkably like a grin. "I fear you are the second person in as many days to remind me of my misspent youth, Uncle. I can only beg you not let it get around. I doubt my reputation could stand it."

"And a good thing, if you ask me. Why do you do it, come to that? Encourage this ridiculous reputation as the devil, I mean."

His lordship shrugged and spread the tails of his coat to take a seat. "Vanity, no doubt," he admitted truthfully. "That and a certain natural misanthropy. At any rate, it occasionally has its uses."

"As in the slaying of dragons?" guessed his uncle shrewdly.

"Precisely."

"Who else has been recalling your misspent youth to you? You said I was the second."

"Charles Heybridge. He was threatening to pop my cork for me."

His uncle grunted. "I shouldn't suppose he can do it anymore now than he could when you was boys. But I must confess I never understood what the two of you saw in each other. Wouldn't have thought you had a thought in common."

"Perhaps that was the attraction. All I know is that the

friendship has endured," his lordship said with a shrug.

Roddy busied himself with getting his pipe going to his satisfaction. "Seen the *Morning Post*?" he asked idly between puffs. "Where's that rascally waiter, by the by? Never one about when you want one."

"No. I was out rather early today. Should I have?"

"Just wondered. Thought it might have something to do with the slaying of dragons."

The tolerant amusement in his lordship's face abruptly fled, and he almost snatched up the paper at his uncle's elbow, already turned to the court page. What he read there was enough to turn his expression to fury, making him look the very devil he was called.

"Who's the gel?" inquired his uncle, regarding these changes with some interest. "Had no idea young Heybridge was on the verge of getting riveted."

"Hell and the devil confound her to eternal flames!" swore his lordship violently, ignoring his uncle. "So she thinks the first round has gone to her, does she? She will soon enough learn her mistake."

"Who is she?" repeated his uncle. "Do I know her?"

"She is," pronounced his lordship through his teeth, "a beautiful, unconscionable doxie! She obviously thinks this will checkmate me, but she doesn't yet know me. I will show her just how toothless my threats are."

"Once the engagement's been puffed off in all the papers, it will be damned awkward if not impossible for young Heybridge to draw back," Roddy said, shrugging. "I'd say she had you, m'boy."

"She has not wed him yet," snapped his lordship. "Nor will she if I have anything to do with it."

"Aye, but it's a dangerous game to come between a friend and the woman he loves," observed Roddy placidly. "Take my word for it. If you're proved right, the friend will hate you for it; and if you're wrong, he'll feel the same. You can't win."

Deveril gave a harsh laugh. "Don't try to convince me you ever in your life did anything so energetic, Roddy. And for your information, Charles is about to wed the grand-daughter of Barbara Foxcroft."

Roderick's jaw dropped open, though not, perhaps, for quite the reason his nephew had intended. "Good God!" he said, sitting up. "Now there's a name to take one back. Barbara Foxcroft. Lord, I haven't thought of her in years."

"I take it, from this display of idiocy, that you knew her?"

"Knew her? Of course I knew her," snorted Roderick. "She led us all a merry chase, I can tell you. A little before my time, but I was no more immune than anyone else, I fear. In fact, most bewitching creature I ever saw. Lord, to think of her being a grandmother! It makes me feel my age, that's what it does. Damned depressing."

"God! It needed only that!" pronounced his lordship savagely. "The picture of you bestirring yourself to pay languid court to the king's mistress is too nauseating at any hour, but especially before breakfast."

"No, no, that's putting too fine a point on it," insisted his uncle, uninsulted. "Told you she was before my time. Only saw her a few times, and she wouldn't have wasted a glance on me. Younger son and all that. She was far more ambitious. I remember old Hanbury—"

"Pray spare me this no doubt delightful stroll down memory lane," begged his lordship acidly. "I have not the slightest desire to hear of her many conquests."

But Roddy was lost in the mists of nostalgia and seemed not to hear him. "Most bewitching creature I ever saw, even then. Not coarse at all, you know. She could drink most men under the table, or so I understand, and win a fortune off you at cards, but she still managed to make drooling idiots of all who saw her. More, she was as shrewd as she was ambitious. When she and the king parted at last he settled a handsome sum on her, and she managed to turn it into a fortune, so I understand. Built that showplace of hers as well, no doubt to rub the noses of the disapproving in her success. Dear, dear. Barbara Foxcroft. Who'd have thought it? Is the granddaughter anything like her?''

"You must forgive me if I fail to follow your example and lapse into idiocy," snapped his nephew. "But having never set eyes on Barbara Foxcroft I can't say. She certainly would appear to be as ambitious. Only her price seems to be marriage this time."

Roddy waved aside these unimportant details. "No, no, I don't care for that. What does she look like, you fool?"

His lordship shrugged, making an effort to control his temper. "Oh, she is beautiful enough, in all conscience. She has the coloring of a Botticelli Venus, a passionate mouth, a determined chin, and eyes that seem to look right through you. She even possesses surprising intelligence for one of her stamp. Whether it is enough to get her what she wants still remains to be seen."

His uncle's eyes had begun to gleam slightly, but he merely pointed out logically, "If she's anything like her grandmother, I wouldn't underestimate her. But why Charles? That's what has me puzzled. I mean, nothing to say against the boy, but he's by no means a prize catch. In her day her grandmother wouldn't have looked twice at him."

"Either she's playing a very deep game, or she has indeed determined upon marriage, in which case Charles would seem to be the perfect candidate," answered his lordship cynically. "He's hopelessly impressionable where women are concerned and has a long history of tilting at windmills to rescue distressed damsels. Anyone wealthier—or less chivalric—would never consider offering her marriage and she knows it. I will concede she is being unexpectedly clever.''

Then he set his teeth together with something of a snap. ''But she has reckoned without me, I fear. For all her cleverness, Miss Christina Castleford will soon rue so direct a challenge. I will admit the first honors go to her, for she must have known this morning that the engagement was to be announced today, and gave no hint of it. But she will soon discover I am not a man to be trifled with lightly.''

''Aye, want her for yourself, don't you?'' inquired his uncle, grinning.

My lord raised suddenly narrowed eyes to his uncle's face. ''I am not disputing this masterful assumption,'' he said politely after a moment. ''But I am curious what makes you think so, Uncle?''

''Lord, I'm not in my dotage yet,'' protested Roddy, still grinning. ''Only stands to reason. At any rate, all this vicarious indignation don't quite fit your reputation, I fear. Young Heybridge is fully of age. If he's stuck his neck in parson's mousetrap, any friend of his would regret it, but it would go no further. Ergo, you want the chit for yourself.''

When Deveril made no answer, he went on cheerfully, ''But it seems to me you've little enough to worry about. I've no desire to add to your already overweening vanity, my boy, but young Heybridge lacks both your wealth and your title. As for the rest, he's an attractive youth, but he don't possess your dark fascination for the ladies. You must know that as well as I, for modesty was never one of your long suits.''

After a moment Deveril shrugged. ''Unfortunately I have no intention of offering her marriage, and she knows it.''

''Well, I daresay even you must jib at the notion of

marrying her to Charles and enjoying her anyway,'' said his uncle frankly. ''But have you no compunction about taking away your best friend's fiancée and making her your mistress?'' He sounded merely idly curious.

His lordship's mouth twisted. ''Very little. She is, after all, admirably suited to the role I have designed for her, but she will make Charles a damnable wife. I'd be doing him a favor. She may be beautiful, but she's a heartless jade who will undoubtedly ruin him in the end. At any rate, he'll soon get over it. You know his brief fascinations never last long.''

His uncle merely grunted. ''Knowing you, I take it you have some hold over her?''

''A slight one,'' conceded Deveril reluctantly. ''Enough to break her marriage with Charles. Not enough to force her to turn to me.''

''Then use it,'' recommended his uncle cynically. ''If she can't have Charles, she'd be a fool not to leap at your offer.''

Again his lordship hesitated. ''You may be right,'' he said at last. ''But I discover I have an odd dislike of such crude methods. I will admit that she stirs my blood as no woman has done in a very long while. It may be quixotic of me, but when she comes to me I would prefer it to be of her own free will.''

''Such scruples no doubt do you honor, m'boy,'' snorted his uncle, ''but I fear they are probably misplaced. If you ask me, this engagement is designed merely to force your offer up. She's Barbara Foxcroft's granddaughter, ain't she?''

''You may be right, but I somehow doubt it. I told you she was intelligent. And doubtless she has had a lifetime of living with the more dubious results of her grandmother's notoriety to learn what she wants. For her purposes, I will concede that marriage to Charles would be the perfect solution. He would give her nominal acceptance while being far too good-natured to suspect her ulterior motives or any subsequent infidelities. Oh, yes, she has been damnably clever, curse her beautiful, warped soul.''

"Then use your tool against her," repeated Roddy, beginning to yawn. "If it's marriage she's after, it seems to me it's the only way you'll get her. Charles certainly can't cry off now without laying himself open to a suit for breach of promise at the very least, and you've said you won't take her once she is married to Charles. If you want her, it's your only choice. You may feel a certain squeamishness at the time, but it will soon pass, believe me," he added callously.

"This insight into your morals is most enlightening, Uncle," drawled his lordship. "But don't make Miss Castleford's mistake of underestimating me. I am not refraining from forcing her into my arms merely out of a misguided sense of chivalry. Were I to do so it would, indeed, put an end to my friendship with Charles, and that, oddly enough, I am loath to do.''

"Then give her up," recommended Roddy, by now bored with the problem.

"That also I am oddly loath to do. But while Charles may not end the relationship, she can. And by the time I'm through with her she will count it a relief to escape and come to me.''

"What do you mean to do?" inquired his uncle curiously.

Deveril smiled. It was the smile Miss Castleford most disliked. "I don't yet know," he admitted. "But I have every faith that events will play into my hands. She has had it all her own way so far, and has been able to bewitch Charles with her beautiful, tragic eyes. I know well just how to show her true colors sooner or later, and I have every intention of, er, helping the process along. She should have whisked him off to Gretna Green while she had the chance. Failing that, she will never wed him.''

His uncle was regarding him with some fascination. "Damme, you did indeed look like a devil just then, m'boy. I almost have it in me to pity the poor girl."

"You need not," said his lordship cynically. "She deserves everything that is undoubtedly coming to her."

Chapter 7

IF MISS CASTLEFORD had advanced an unexpectedly bold pawn in her first move, Deveril was soon able to counter it very thoroughly.

When he returned home that afternoon he ruthlessly sifted through the invitation cards that had piled up in his absence and deliberately selected one from a minor hostess who was a great friend of Lady Danbury's and might be depended upon to receive that matron's new protegée.

He also spent a profitable hour culling what gossip he could about the new beauty. He was amply rewarded for his pains, for what he learned was more than enough to justify his opinion of her. It seemed she had received the cut direct from a number of more notable hostesses, and had not a prayer of being admitted to that holy of holies, Almack's. She had understandably received considerable notice from the male half of the *ton*, but generally her assault upon London society was seen as an insult. Oh, yes, a fine wife she would make for Charles, thought Deveril sardonically.

But despite Miss Castleford's skepticism, he had no intention of making the mistake of saying so again to Charles. His uncle was right. Coming between a man and the object of his even transient desire was to court disaster and play right into the lady's hands. No, Miss Castleford must be made to break off the engagement herself. She had shown herself overconfident in so direct a challenge. She would very soon be made to realize her mistake.

He therefore presented himself at Mrs. Maitland's house at a fashionably late hour that evening, and endured an almost fawning welcome with only a slight curl to his lip.

When he at length managed to escape from her, his contempt only increased as he made his way across the ballroom. The company was far from select, being comprised largely of the shabby-genteel, wealthy Cits, and mushrooms. So this was what Charles was to be fated to in future? It was one weapon to use against her, for while Charles was no snob he was used to mixing in the first circles. Miss Castleford would have to be beautiful indeed to long blind him to the disadvantages of her situation.

He soon was rewarded by sight of his quarry at the end of the room. Charles was looking slightly uncomfortable but making a valient effort not to show it. He was listening politely to something Lady Danbury was saying in his ear, but his eyes were on a rather vulgar beauty in an elaborate toilette who was ogling him quite openly from nearby.

But at least there was nothing vulgar, at least outwardly, about his fiancée, curse her mercenary little soul. Miss Castleford was even looking particularly ravishing that evening, reveling no doubt in her recent victory. His lordship had to concede reluctantly that her taste was excellent, for she affected a quietly simple elegance that underplayed rather than overplayed her unusual coloring.

Tonight she had even had the audacity to attire herself in a simple gown of white gauze over a satin underslip, eschewing no other ornament than a silver fillip in that remarkable hair of hers. She managed to look, despite every expectation to the contrary, unexpectedly pure and innocent.

Certainly every other lady in that lowly assembly tended to look overdressed by comparison.

Deveril's expression grew even more unpleasantly saturnine as he unwillingly applauded her nerve and instincts. She was clever, all right, he had to give her that. Just not quite clever enough.

Charles caught sight of him then and beckoned delightedly. So, she had not told Charles of their meeting that morning. That was interesting, and revealed more to him than she knew. She had scored a minor victory by getting the betrothal announced so quickly, but it would not save her. The next trick would definitely be his own.

She saw him then, and he had the satisfaction of seeing her lips tighten and her eyes begin to flash. But she did not cower or betray any fear, to give her her due. Her chin merely came up and she stood waiting for him to reach them, defiance in every line of her slim, elegant figure. Deveril had been right to think he was going to enjoy every minute of the coming struggle between them.

Charles, true to form, betrayed no suspicion that anything was in the least wrong. "Dev! I had no expectations of seeing you here," he exclaimed delightedly. "Have you come to wish me happy? I take it you saw the announcement this morning?"

Deveril could not resist casting Miss Castleford a brief, scathing glance. She returned it with interest. "Certainly," he returned mildly. "When is the wedding to be?"

"Soon. Neither of us sees any reason to wait."

"Don't you?" inquired his lordship, casting a glance of acute dislike at Miss Castleford. "I hope I am to be invited?"

He had expected triumph on Miss Castleford's face, but he saw only distrust and a certain amount of puzzlement. It was clear she had not expected this calm acceptance from him.

That suited him very well, but Charles's next words had the effect of jerking his attention back and wiping the somewhat smug expression off his face. "Yes, of course you are invited," he said somewhat doubtfully. "But we are to be married abroad, you know."

He had all of Deveril's attention now. "Abroad?" his lordship repeated quickly, his eyes sweeping in sudden suspicion to Christina's.

"Yes, I want to take Christina to Brussels," said Charles innocently. "She's never been abroad, and has no great love for London. I told you she would make an excellent farmer's wife. I need not fear she will be longing to be back in town all the time."

Deveril's eyes took on something of a malicious gleam, for he had little doubt why Miss Castleford disliked London. She must be unpleasantly reminded every day of society's lack of welcome and endure a good many cuts and rude comments. It was little wonder she longed to escape.

But Charles was going on happily: "We mean to be married over there. With the conference and all, it seemed the perfect time. Luckily Lady Danbury has kindly agreed to go with us as chaperone."

"I see," remarked his lordship, his eyes once more on Miss Castleford's beautiful, treacherous face. "And when do you embark on this journey?"

"Oh, as soon as possible, I think. Lady Danbury thinks she can be ready in a fortnight. I have looked out the packets already and written to obtain lodgings in Brussels. There seems to be no problem about being married over there."

"This is indeed a coincidence," remarked his lordship blandly. "As it happens, I was thinking of going abroad myself. Perhaps we should join forces. *Devil's Lady* is berthed at Southampton, and I suspect Miss Castleford and her ladyship will find her far more comfortable than the public packet.''

"Why, that's famous!" exclaimed Charles. "You must know the *Devil's Lady* is his yacht, my dear. She is worth a fortune and puts every other private ship into the shade," he said to Christina. "Blaise once won a fabulous wager by crossing the Channel in her in six hours."

Deveril paid little attention, for he had had the reward of seeing Christina start, her blue eyes opening wide in unmistakable alarm. Doubtlessly part of her sudden dislike of London had to do with his presence there, and if so he had countered her pawn most effectively.

To her credit she tried valiantly to squirm out of this latest trap. "I am sure it is delightful," she said in her attractively husky voice, "but we couldn't possibly think of imposing so on his lordship. Besides, have you forgotten, Charles, that Robin is thinking of coming as well? I feel sure our party will be too large even for Lord Deveril's yacht."

Deveril smiled knowingly at her. "Nonsense, Miss Castleford," he said, enjoying himself. "Besides, it will give me an opportunity to become better acquainted with you. After all, once you are married we will be seeing a good deal of each other."

She looked as if she would have liked to throw something at him, but Charles agreed with his ready enthusiasm, "Yes, that's true. You must know, my dear, that Blaise and I grew up together. He knows more about me than I daresay anyone, and vice versa, I suppose. At any rate, you will like *Devil's Lady*. Blaise and I once spent a summer sailing her, and I never enjoyed anything more. Of course, I'm not the seaman Deveril is, for I'm strictly a fair-weather sailor, I fear. But the Channel should be fairly calm this time of year."

"Have you sailed before, Miss Castleford?" inquired his lordship.

Her eyes struck daggers through him. "No. And I am not at all sure I can be ready to leave in a fortnight. I have ordered a great many things which may not be ready in time."

He bowed with a mockery only she could detect. "It makes no odds, I assure you. I have no definite plans and am entirely at your disposal."

"Then that's settled," said Charles happily. "I have been meaning to ask you, in fact, Dev, if I should hire a courier to send over before us? I don't fear any trouble, of course, but I want to make the journey as comfortable as possible."

"That shouldn't be necessary," drawled his lordship. "I will send my agent to make any necessary arrangements. In fact, you may as well leave everything to me. You need only tell me the appointed day and I will undertake to do the rest."

"Lord, if Dev is to take care of everything, I know we shall have nothing to worry about," laughed Charles. "You must know he spends a fortune insuring his own comfort, my dear. We shall literally have nothing to do but pack our bags and present ourselves on the appointed day."

Miss Castleford was betrayed into closing her mouth with something perilously close to a snap.

Christina, indeed gnashing her teeth over this latest development, had perforce to accept that Lord Deveril had shown depressing promptitude in reacting to her challenge. She had no idea what he hoped to accomplish by this unexpected move, but she did not need to be told that such a journey under Deveril's management and demonic eye would be extremely unpleasant.

She still did not believe even he would dare carry through with the more drastic of his threats, for they did not live in the Dark Ages, after all. He might wish to strangle her, but despite his reputation he was not supernatural and must abide by the laws that governed the rest of them.

Even so, she did not deceive herself that he was not a

dangerous enemy. He might inexplicably have refrained from using his strongest weapon against her, but he had made it clear that he had no intention of backing down and accepting a fait accompli. How it would all end was anybody's guess.

Nor did it do any good to rail against the unfairness of fate. It might seem wickedly unjust that Deveril had judged her on no more than her name and a moment's aberration, and constituted himself her bitterest enemy. But she had long resigned herself to the innate unfairness of a callous world. Life had taught her that she would have to fight for everything she got, for it was exceedingly unlikely anything would be given to her else.

Well, respectability was what she sought, and she had always known she would have to pay a price for that ambition. Whether the price was too high was yet to be determined. If she insisted upon marrying Charles in the teeth of Deveril's threats, at the very least she might alienate the two friends. At the worst she faced an unpleasant struggle she might lose with a man she was fast learning to fear.

But she also knew that were she to give Charles up, she would undoubtedly face the same struggle with someone else who objected to a closer tie with the granddaughter of the notorious Barbara Foxcroft. She had long ago acknowledged the unpalatable truth of that and deliberately hardened her heart. It might seem that a modicum of happiness and security seemed little enough to ask out of life, but clearly the cynical world thought differently. It condemned out of hand the women who led such a life as her grandmother, but effectively barred them from ever escaping it.

At any rate, even if she were to consider giving Charles up—as she would admit had occurred to her—more practical considerations intruded. She was fast running out of both time and money, and were she to return to her grandmother unsuccessful, she would have little ammunition left with which to withstand that formidable lady's scarcely disguised blackmail. When stacked against her grandmother's prime candidate for her hand, Charles Heybridge must appear a positive paragon of virtue by comparison.

It was perhaps a desperate gamble now that Deveril had arrived on the scene. And if she failed? Well, marriage was not her only option, after all. She was hardheaded enough to have considered other possibilities as well. Nor was she dependent upon her grandmother to rescue her. She might fend for herself if need be. The fact that the limited choices before her in that case were all of them uniformly depressing, ranging from menial domestic work to setting herself up as a rival to her grandmother, might in the end have to be overlooked—especially if Lord Deveril had his way.

As for accepting Deveril's, or some other man's, dishonorable proposal, she knew with cynical honesty that she was neither particularly horrified at the thought, nor considered herself morally any better than her grandmother had been. Given Barbara Foxcroft's options at the time and the drawbacks of her poverty-stricken background, her grandmother had done very well indeed for herself. She had successfully parlayed her face and her ambition into enslaving a king and achieving a fortune for herself, and few women could claim as much.

The problem was that Christina had long realized that such a life was not for her. Deveril had obviously considered that his offer must tempt her, but she had not even considered it. He would no doubt set her up in handsome style, and she would even achieve a certain distinction, for Deveril was a noted connoisseur if Charles were to be believed.

Unfortunately, a lifetime spent on the edges of the demimonde had shown her that for her the rewards of such a liaison were unlikely to outweigh the liabilities. For all her achievements, Barbara Foxcroft was still a scandalous

byword some forty years later, and her children and grandchildren forced to pay the price of her notoriety.

Indeed, Christina feared she was but a dull creature. Robin
might protest that marriage with Charles would be a tedious
affair, but then she had had enough of drama and emotions
to last her a lifetime. The truth was, she thought she could
conceive of nothing more desirable than spending the rest
of her days in a peaceful backwater, protected from all the
world by an adoring husband.

So. It seemed she fought Deveril. And to tell the truth,
he had made her angry enough that it would have gone very
much against her pluck to give in to his demands. Aside from
everything else she thought it was his hypocrisy that most
disgusted her. From all she could tell, he cared nothing for
his own reputation and lived completely for his own pleasure.
But he was more than ready to blacken her for no more than
an accident of birth. Well, let him do his worst. They would
see who won in the end.

Chapter 8

CHRISTINA did try her best to dissuade Charles from this change in traveling plans. But since she naturally could not reveal the real reason for her objections, she was not much surprised when he dismissed her fears with his usual cheerful optimism.

"Nonsense," he insisted cheerfully. "He wouldn't have offered if he didn't mean it, I promise you. And if you give him a chance, I think you will find Dev very different from his reputation, you know. To be honest, I was surprised and pleased at his offer. And it will indeed give you both an opportunity to become better acquainted."

She might have told him, of course, that they both knew everything about the other they cared to, but resignedly held her tongue. When Charles had first suggested removing to Brussels, where a good part of the world had gone because of the peace conference even then taking place, she had leapt at the suggestion. She had indeed never been abroad, and a quiet wedding there seemed much preferable to one held under the full glare of London's disapproving eye. At any rate, as Deveril had surmised, she had found London society very little to her taste. She would be happy if she never set foot in the place again.

Now she was tempted to tell Charles she had changed her mind. But that seemed a craven capitulation to what were, after all, no more than Deveril's vague threats. At any rate, it seemed too late to draw back now without a very good reason, and she could think of none that would not effectively postpone the wedding as well.

She was even momentarily tempted to confess the whole to Charles and trust in his sense of fair play. She thought he was indeed still besotted enough with her to take her part, even against his oldest friend, and that would effectively spike Deveril's guns forever.

But something held her back. She cared nothing for Deveril, of course, but she had no wish to see Charles wounded by the loss of such an old friend. At any rate, that would be to show herself little better than Deveril thought her. And she had vowed to herself when she first accepted Charles's offer that she did so only as long as he didn't suffer from the engagement. It seemed thus she hoped to salvage her foolish pride in the face of so unequal a match.

Well, she still meant it, and to begin her marriage by asking her husband to choose between her and his oldest friend seemed to betray from the outset the bargain she had made with herself.

It might come to that in the end, of course. But she had an odd reluctance to be the first to force the issue.

By the same token, she briefly considered and then discarded Robin's suggestion that she should marry Charles at once. The gossip such a step would invite would naturally be unpleasant and do much to arouse the scandal she urgently wished to avoid. But it would at least put an end once and for all to Deveril's threats. Even he could hardly set aside a marriage that had already taken place.

But that, too, sat ill with her pride. She feared Robin would accuse her of being too squeamish. She only knew that while she had long ago been forced to acknowledge that marriage with her must bring Charles some notoriety and unpleasantness, at least he should have every opportunity to draw back if he wished. He must walk into the marriage with his eyes open or not at all.

Which left her exactly where she had started. Short of feigning illness at the last minute or withdrawing from the marriage completely, she could see no way of avoiding the coming journey in Deveril's company. And she found it impossible to look forward to it with the same pleasant excitement she had previously known.

But at least Deveril had no immediate new unpleasantness in store for her, for he seemed to be biding his time even as she was. True to his word, he obviously had not told Charles of their meeting at the masked ball, and though they met on several occasions over the next fortnight, he contented himself with looking her over with his mocking, unnatural eyes. There was both a sting and a challenge in his face, but it seemed only she could read it. Charles remained wholly impervious to the tensions between his oldest friend and his fiancée.

In the meantime, preparations for the trip went on apace. Fortunately Robin had indeed decided to join the party, to Christina's undisguised relief. His reasons might have much to do with a desire to be out of London and the reach of his creditors for the appreciable future, and he retained a somewhat amused fascination with the battle raging between his sister and Deveril. But Christina was glad of his support on a journey that promised to be exceedingly unpleasant.

This fear was only increased when Charles's sister, Lucinda, wrote at the last moment begging to be allowed to accompany them. She was at present visiting friends in the north, but pledged herself to reach London in time to set out with them and pronounced herself eager to make the acquaintance of her new sister-in-law to be.

That sounded promising enough, but Christina confessed to herself that she was dreading meeting Miss Heybridge. It was too much to expect that Charles's sister would share his easy indifference to her grandmother's past, and she might be forgiven for resenting Christina heartily.

Indeed, between worry and the necessity to pack both her own and Lady Danbury's trunks, for it seemed she was an indifferent traveler, Christina was in an advanced state of nerves by the time the appointed day arrived. Lady Danbury vacillated endlessly about what she should take and what to leave behind, and ended by packing a large part of her wardrobe and personal possessions. In vain did Christina try to persuade her that French inns were reputed to be highly respectable and she would not need to take her own bed linens, not to mention her own pillows and favorite footstool. Lady Danbury was convinced that no comfort was to be found outside of England, and was determined to be safe rather than sorry.

Nor did the day they were to leave begin on a propitious note. They had agreed to gather at Lady Danbury's at eight, so they might get an early start, but both Robin and Miss Heybridge were more than an hour late, Robin because he had overslept and Miss Heybridge because she had misplaced a vital portmanteau.

Since Charles was fetching his sister, Christina, Lord Deveril, and Lady Danbury were left to cool their heels in awkward conversation while his lordship's horses began to fret and plunge at the delay.

Unfortunately, Deveril himself had been annoyingly prompt, arriving well before the appointed hour and enduring with unexpected patience the delinquency of the rest of the party. Christina had the impression he was merely unpleasantly amused by the morning's mishaps.

To add to the confusion, after Lady Danbury's trunks had been loaded onto the baggage wagon, she bethought herself of some last-minute item she was sure she had forgotten to pack. All of her numerous possessions had had to be unloaded while she searched for the missing item.

Lord Deveril leaned his shoulder against one of the vehicles, his ankles crossed, and sardonically watched while her trunks were fruitlessly ransacked by Christina and her ladyship's harassed maid. It was only when the last had been repacked and strapped up again that the missing item was found in the bottom of her reticule, where she herself had put it.

Christina had spent too many years being responsible for her mother's haphazard method of traveling to be much surprised by this last-minute panic, but she could not help but be annoyed by Deveril's annoyingly supercilious detachment. Nor did it help when Charles confided to her later that Deveril had predicted they would be a full three hours late in starting.

They were not quite that, but it had been a fair estimate. By the time Lady Danbury's boxes had all been reloaded, Miss Heybridge and Charles had arrived. Charles's sister proved to be a delicately pretty blonde, dressed in the height of fashion, and with a pleasing shyness. She was in fact Christina's age, but appeared very much younger. Christina was soon to suspect it was because she possessed a helpless, childlike air that belied her years.

She had a pretty habit of hesitating, then turning her appealing eyes on the nearest male, usually Deveril, as if waiting to be rescued. It seemed to work, for even Deveril was less bitingly sardonic in her company. After five minutes in Miss Heybridge's company Christina began to feel vulgarly overblown by comparison with her vivid coloring and decided manner.

Miss Heybridge embraced Christina, saying in a gentle, rather colorless voice that she was so happy to be gaining a sister at last. But there was little warmth in her manner. Christina had no way of knowing if she had been told of her future sister-in-law's background and disapproved, or simply reserved the greater part of her energy for the male sex. Certainly her eyes followed Deveril in a highly revealing way that verged on adoration.

For his part, Charles seemed extremely fond of his sister, while even Deveril, whom Christina had seen only as a mocking devil, betrayed an unexpectedly softer side to his nature in her presence. He treated her much as an affectionate older brother, teasing her about the amount of luggage she had brought with her and wondering if he should hire another vehicle to carry it all.

Robin appeared only at the last minute astride a raking new chestnut he had recently won at faro and was inordinately proud of. He apologized with a grin for being late, saying he had overslept, for he had a devilish deep night of it, but confessing he had doubted they would set out on time. To Christina's dismay it had been arranged that she, Miss Heybridge, and Lady Danbury were to travel in Deveril's elegant coach with its distinguished crest upon the door. It would undoubtedly be more comfortable than a hired vehicle, but she had no desire to be under any obligation to him. And she soon learned that it lent to their journey a distinction that she could certainly have done without.

Lady Danbury and Miss Heybridge's maids, Charles's and Deveril's valets, and the baggage were to follow in two separate hired vehicles. Deveril was driving himself in his own high-perch phaeton and team of beautiful grays, and Charles could either choose to ride with him or mount his own bay, tied on behind one of the baggage wagons. All in all, it promised to be a ridiculous cavalcade, and Christina found herself yearning for the previous anonymity she had once anticipated.

With the party at last assembled they set out, though it was nearer to noon than breakfast time when they were at last on the road. Counting his lordship's coachman, the postilions, and outriders, it was quite a procession. Christina thought it faintly ridiculous, but it did not seem to occur to either of her companions that to require three vehicles, ten servants, and half their household goods to make a three-day journey was somewhat excessive.

She could tell by Robin's grin that he, at least, appreciated the irony. But unfortunately there was little opportunity to share it with him. Once introduced to Miss Heybridge, he promptly began to flirt outrageously with her, annoying Christina extremely. Only at the last minute, when they were climbing into the coach, did he thrust a sealed packet into his sister's hands, asking her with a grin to keep it safe for him.

There was no time for more, and he annoyed her even more by riding ahead, leaving the slower vehicles far behind. To ride tamely along beside a lumbering coach was extremely tedious, Christina knew, for she was finding the going wearing herself. It appeared that Lady Danbury had a pronounced dislike of being jolted over indifferent roads, and Deveril's coach, exceedingly well sprung and built for speed, was forced to crawl at a pace that suited her notions of comfortable travel.

Lucinda proved to be a pleasant enough traveling companion, though she had very little to say and tended to keep her eye on the window where Deveril and her brother could be seen, politely keeping company with them. At the first two halts Robin proved singularly elusive, and somehow there was not a moment for her to have a private word with him. It was not until late in the afternoon that she was able to corner him and demand an explanation of the strange packet. And then his answer was glib enough to arouse all her worst suspicions.

"It's nothing you need worry about," he told her, grinning. "Just a private piece of business."

"Business?" she frowned. "What kind of business?"

He looked briefly annoyed. "Do I interfere in your affairs? Even when you affianced yourself to the dull but worthy Charles? Though his sister's pretty enough, I'll admit. This trip may prove more enjoyable than I'd imagined."

She was easily sidetracked by this new fear, as perhaps he'd known she would be. "Leave his sister alone," she snapped, well acquainted with her brother. Then she forced her mind back to the subject at hand. "And don't try to fob me off. What business? I distrust you in your present mood."

"What you don't know won't upset you," Robin assured her, returned to good humor. "Don't forget it was you who forbade me to put the touch to my dear brother-in-law to be. You can't complain when I'm forced to raise the ready in any way I can."

She could get no more out of him and had too many worries of her own to press him further. At any rate he was probably right. The less she knew the better.

Deveril observed this private conversation between brother and sister with a faint disapproving scowl. Miss Lucinda Heybridge, who had come up behind him, remarked in her colorless way, "They are very much alike, aren't they? Charles had told me they were twins, of course, but I was startled to see them together for the first time."

He turned to regard her, his rather saturnine expression very much in evidence. "Very," he agreed dryly.

"They are both very handsome, of course, if you like that

bold style," added Miss Heybridge, arching a look up at him.

His eyes revealed nothing of his thoughts. "No doubt, if you do," he answered uncommunicatively and turned away, leaving her to stare after him in a certain satisfaction.

By the next halt Christina was beginning to envy her brother his freedom. Lucinda and Lady Danbury were both soon dozing and the excitement of the beginning of the journey long since worn off. Christina sat gazing out of the window, her back to the horses, feeling bored and depressed. She did not suffer from carriage sickness herself, as both Lady Danbury and Lucinda seemed prone to. But traveling for hours invariably gave her a headache, and she would have much preferred to be out in the fresh air to clear it.

At the next halt, she gratefully stretched her legs, and drank the lemonade Charles obtained for them, declining the macaroons and cakes. Lucinda had woken up refreshed and hungry, and ate several of the macaroons.

Charles came to smile warmly down at Christina. "Are you very weary of the journey already?" he inquired in concern. "Dev insisted we could easily have made Dover in one day, but I didn't want to push it. My sister never travels well, I fear. How are you getting along, by the way?"

Christina, aware of Deveril's mocking eyes on her, could only answer him stiffly, and was glad enough to climb back into the coach again.

Deveril stopped to speak to his coachman, who looked first uncomfortable, then impassive. As Lucinda started to follow Christina back into the coach Deveril stepped forward and smiled down at her, saying something in a low voice.

Christina, blinded by the unexpected charm of that smile, was aware of a certain bitterness in her heart.

Deveril next spoke to Charles, who looked surprised but then nodded. A moment later, Robin sauntered over to the open door of the coach to announce, "Deveril has suggested that Miss Heybridge's queasiness will be improved by going in his phaeton for part of the way. She will rejoin you at the next halt.''

Despite herself Christina's bitterness returned. Miss Heybridge's every need was to be instantly taken care of, it seemed, while her own nagging headache was of little importance.

Then she was promptly ashamed of herself for her pettiness, and tried to ignore the laughter and the chatter she could hear from just outside the window of the stuffy coach once they had started.

Deveril soon pulled ahead, Charles on horseback beside him, and it was not long before they disappeared from sight. But Robin hung back for once, seeming to become belatedly aware of his duty to his sister. He chatted desultorily through the open window of the coach, beginning to yawn and complaining of the tediousness of the day. He was half sorry he had come, for to be riding at a snail's pace along a tame English road, escorting a family party when he might have been back in London amusing himself had quickly begun to pall.

If so, the tedium was soon to be broken in no uncertain terms, for they had just rounded a bend in the road when there was an unexpected jolt. The heavy coach wheels climbed up the bank on one side of the road, throwing both occupants sideways, as if the horses were bolting with them. The next instant with an ominous crack it had lurched ponderously down again, coming to rest at an awkward angle, the coach's off door buried deep in the hedge and the other facing the sky.

Chapter 9

LADY DANBURY AND CHRISTINA, wholly unprepared for this catastrophe, were both tumbled violently onto the floor. For a moment all was confusion, the horses plunging, the coachman swearing, and Lady Danbury uttering dazed sounds of distress.

It was impossible to tell if she were hurt or not, for she was beyond coherence. As impossible as it was to right themselves in the deeply canted vehicle. The seats were now virtually upright and the off door where the roof should have been.

For her part, Christina was aware of bruised knees and elbows and a vague sense of disbelief, but she made an effort to scramble off poor Lady Danbury, who was now beginning to moan pitiably.

"Good God, are you hurt, ma'am?" she demanded, righting herself with the greatest difficulty and trying to pull her companion up off the floor.

Even at her words the free door was jerked open, and Robin's face appeared above them. "Kit! Are you all right?"

"Yes, yes! Only get us out of here."

The coachman had appeared by this time, his face very red and apologetic. "Is anyone hurt?"

"If they aren't, it's no thanks to you!" Robin snapped, venting his alarm. "What the devil do you mean overturning the coach like that?"

The coachman turned even redder. "It was unavoidable," he muttered sullenly. "A rabbit ran across the road and startled one of the leaders."

"A rabbit?" cried Robin, justifiably incensed. "Well, if you ask me, it was a damned cow-handed piece of driving! They might both have been killed."

"Oh, what does it matter?" Christina cried. "See to Lady Danbury, Robin. We can discuss it when we are all on solid ground again." She was aware of a delayed reaction of fright in herself that seemed absurd, since the danger was now past.

Between them Robin and the coachman managed to pull Lady Danbury out, but it was an indelicate operation in no way helped by the lady herself, who had gone alarmingly limp. She endured the indignity of being jerked bodily out of the door by her arms and collapsed on the roadway in mounting hysterics.

While they tended to her, Christina managed to extricate herself by means of tucking up her skirts and pulling herself out. She emerged to discover the horses in disorder, the coachman listening sullenly to Robin's diatribe, and that, as if to add to the general misery, it had begun to lightly drizzle.

Maddeningly, there was no sign of Charles or Deveril's phaeton, and the two vehicles carrying the servants and baggage had inexplicably fallen behind and were nowhere in sight. Christina was left to deal with the hysterical Lady Danbury in the middle of the road in the rain.

She managed to find the latter's smelling salts, but they seemed to have little effect. Christina said irritably to her brother, who was still inclined to determine the blame, "Oh, for heaven's sake, leave the poor man alone, Robin, and do something constructive. We shall both be soaked in a moment.''

Robin reluctantly broke off to take belated stock of their situation and angrily ordered that umbrellas should be found at once. But it soon appeared that the umbrellas had been packed in one of the baggage vehicles, for they were nowhere to be found.

Christina was beyond emotion by then. "Never mind," she interrupted the groom trying to explain this curious lack of forethought. "One of you find something to shield Lady Danbury with, then we'll see what's to be done with the coach."

A rug from the cantilevered coach was quickly fetched, and a makeshift shelter made for Lady Danbury, who showed no signs of abating her hysterics. Christina wrapped herself in another rug, seeing no reason to become soaked herself, and regretfully abandoned her chaperone to see to more practical needs.

These were quickly shown to be mostly futile. It was soon discovered that the right front wheel had been smashed beyond repair, and it was unlikely that the coach would be righted until the wheel was repaired.

It seemed preferable for Lady Danbury to re-enter it to catching her death of cold, so she was bundled back inside, out of the cold rain.

Robin was still inclined to be incensed over what he saw as an inexcusable piece of bad driving. The coachman endured his complaints with a heightened color, but disdained making any further excuses, though the other servants showed signs of becoming restive. Realizing it, Christina at last broke in wearily, "Oh, leave it, Robin. What does it matter why we overturned?"

"What does it matter, when Lady Danbury is in hysterics and we're left to catch our death in the rain?" demanded

Robin, his resentment increasing. "And all because of a piece of cow-handed driving I'm surprised a man as demanding as Deveril would tolerate. I shall have a few words to say to his lordship, you may be sure."

"I am more concerned where the baggage coaches can have gotten to. Do you know, Blackaby?" asked Christina of the coachman.

But he was oddly unforthcoming on that subject as well. "I'm sure I couldn't say, miss. They were behind us at the last stop."

"Well, they aren't now," snorted Robin. "And where the devil are Deveril and Heybridge, if it comes to that? Probably taken shelter in some inn to wait the rain out, if I know them."

It soon began to seem as if he were right. The postilion offered to unhitch one of the team and ride for help, but neither of the following baggage coaches made an appearance, nor did Deveril's phaeton return to see what was keeping them. Robin paced back and forth angrily along the side of the road in the rain, swearing under his breath, while Christina, by now thoroughly wet and chilled, at last retired again to the coach to wait, despite its awkward angle.

She found that Lady Danbury's hysterics had finally abated, only to be replaced by a strong attack of indignation and self-pity. She alternated by abusing Deveril's coachman and describing in finite detail the lasting harm she had undoubtedly suffered. On the whole, Christina would have preferred to stand in the rain than be obliged to soothe her ruffled sensibilities, but there was no help for it, of course.

Almost an hour passed before the sounds of an arrival at last reached them. Christina peered out the window to discover Deveril and Charles had reappeared in Deveril's phaeton, Charles at least looking shocked and gratifyingly upset at the scene they discovered.

She emerged from the uneven coach in time to hear him saying in dismay, "But what on earth caused you to overturn, Blackaby?"

"Exactly my sentiments, Heybridge," retorted Robin.

Charles saw her then and hurried to her. "Christina, you are not hurt? Good God, I can't tell you how sorry I am. We had gone on ahead, you know, and when it came on to rain, we decided to await you in an inn a few miles on. I couldn't have been more shocked when Deveril's servant came to tell us what had happened. Can you ever forgive me, my darling?"

He had taken her hands warmly in his own, and now added guiltily, "Poor angel, you're soaked through and half frozen. I should be horsewhipped for riding on and leaving you."

For some reason Christina looked not at Charles's concerned face but at Deveril's unpleasantly mocking one. She flushed at the dislike she saw there and turned quickly back to Charles. "Never mind. We are none of us hurt, though poor Lady Danbury is sadly shaken, I fear. The sooner we can get her warm and dry the better."

Charles looked stricken. "No doubt, but I'm afraid the inn we were at was a poor one, and they had no vehicle we could hire. We have left Lucinda there, of course, though I disliked having to leave her alone. But the landlord assured me she would be perfectly safe. Deveril's man has gone on ahead to find another coach, but it may be some time before he returns, I fear."

He looked around him then, as if only then remembering their existence and added in astonishment, "But where are the baggage wagons?"

"Your guess is as good as mine," inserted Robin. "We haven't seen hide or hair of 'em."

Deveril had remained silent until then, conferring with his coachman and ignoring the rest of them, but now he said calmly, "Trying to discover what happened to them now seems a waste of energy, I fear. It seems to me that we have two choices. We can remove the ladies to the same inn in my phaeton, though they will be uncomfortably crowded and wet; or they can remain here until a covered vehicle of some sort can be discovered and fetched. Which do you prefer, Miss Castleford?"

Christina knew strongly which one she preferred, but she also knew it was unlikely to jibe with Lady Danbury's choice. The coach might be uncomfortable and by now increasingly cold and damp, but it was undoubtedly preferable in Lady Danbury's view to being obliged to travel some miles in an open and dangerous sporting phaeton in a chilling rain.

In this Lady Danbury quickly concurred, when the choice was presented to her, saying with a strong shudder, that nothing would prevail upon her to set out in Deveril's phaeton.

"I would myself prefer a brief discomfort to several hours of chilled waiting," observed Deveril in a bored voice, "but it is your decision, of course. If you intend to wait with her, Miss Castleford, I would suggest you get back in the coach. You are bedraggled enough as it is."

Christina glared at him with bottled-up resentment for thus reminding her what a sorry spectacle she must make. But Charles said quickly, "Yes, don't stand out here any longer. If you should catch a chill I would never forgive myself."

Christina allowed herself to be returned to the uncomfortable coach, wondering why her nature was obviously so perverse that Charles's touching concern mattered less to her than Deveril's obvious disdain.

The three men stood about for some time, evidently trying to reach a decision. Charles looked miserable, Robin cold and annoyed, and Deveril untouched either by the rain or the situation. At last it was decided that Charles would remain with the ladies, and Deveril and Robin drive on ahead to hasten the rescue. The decision was relayed by Charles, who came to stand by the coach and speak to Christina in a low voice.

He declined to enter the coach, saying that he was too wet and pointing out quite rightly that he would only be catapulted into one of their laps if he tried to sit on the angled seat.

Christina was by then cold and weary and impatient, but it seemed unkind to take her ill temper out on him. At any rate, he was undoubtedly colder and wetter than she was, and so she made lighthearted conversation with him for the next half hour while they once more waited.

She might have spared herself the effort. She could tell by his attitude that Charles would have preferred her to have been as overcome as Lady Danbury had been, in need of a strong shoulder to cry on. She knew already that he was strongly romantic, and used no doubt to his sister's clinging ways, for he seemed to find her humorous matter-of-factness slightly disconcerting. Christina recognized it but thought that at the moment she was beyond putting herself through the exhausting show of helpless femininity he obviously desired.

They were at last rescued, Deveril returning alone in a hired vehicle of some decrepitude. He explained that Robin had remained to keep Lucinda company, and if Christina was made slightly uneasy by this arrangement, distrusting her brother where young and pretty females were concerned, Charles seemed to find nothing amiss in it.

She and Lady Danbury, who had fallen into a light doze, thankfully transferred to the new vehicle, which smelled unmistakably of damp and onions, and were at last conveyed to the small inn Charles and Deveril had spoken of. There still had been no sign of the missing baggage or servants.

Lucinda was discovered before the fire eating toasted

muffins and laughing over something Robin had been saying. He, too, had dried out and looked well pleased with himself, which increased Christina's uneasiness.

Lucinda exclaimed at the sight of them and inadvertently added to Christina's self-consciousness by saying sympathetically, "Oh, you poor thing! You look wet and half frozen! Was there ever so absurd a mishap? Robin says Blackaby swerved to avoid a rabbit or some such thing."

Christina did not miss the fact that Lucinda and her wretched brother seemed to have reached first-name basis already. Robin shot her a wicked glance, but at the moment she had more pressing matters to attend to. "Charles, pray obtain a bedchamber for Lady Danbury, where she can get out of her wet clothes and lie down for a little while," she said wearily. "I'm sure she is exhausted."

But it seemed Robin had already done so. Christina took her up, helped her to remove her damp dress and crawl between the warmed sheets, then made her drink a dose of sal volatile for her shattered nerves, thoughtfully provided by the kindly landlady. Then she returned wearily downstairs, longing only to follow her chaperone's example.

There she found a debate still raging. Charles insisted strongly that they should remain there for the night, seconded by Lucinda, who had taken a liking to the quaint inn. But Deveril pointed out practically that their luggage and dry clothing were probably awaiting them at their destination, and that the small inn was unlikely to be big enough to put them all up at once.

Seeing Christina, Charles immediately appealed to her. Aware of Deveril's hateful glance at her, she answered rather shortly, "I am sure Lady Danbury is exhausted and would be better off here. But since she is already convinced the sheets are damp, and seems to have taken a dislike to the place, and since his lordship is right that we none of us have anything but the clothes we stand up in, I vote that we continue on as soon as possible.''

"Yes, but we've nothing but that miserable vehicle you came in, remember," said Charles apologetically.

"All the more reason. In Maidstone we should be able to hire a better vehicle." She glanced unwillingly at Deveril. "I am assuming that is what you intend to do, my lord? Or do you not care to leave your coach behind?''

He shrugged. "It little matters. If we can obtain a repair to the wheel I feel you and Miss Heybridge will be more comfortable. But that is for you to decide. But are we agreed, then, that we should press on tonight? In that case, as soon as Lady Danbury wakens, we will continue.''

Since no one demurred, that was the plan they followed. Charles insisted that Christina return upstairs and get out of her wet things, which were obligingly cleaned and dried by the landlady. Christina was beginning to feel her many aches and bruises and longed only to crawl between the sheets herself, but Deveril was right. They were but an hour or so from their destination for the night, a comfortable establishment catering to the upper classes, and hopefully their baggage with all their night things would be waiting there for them.

But by the time they were once more on the road, it was after nine when they at last reached Maidstone and pulled up at the comfortable inn Deveril had bespoken rooms in. With Charles's help Christina climbed down stiffly from the uncomfortable hired vehicle, whose springs were vastly inferior to Deveril's coach, and escaped gladly inside, longing only for a cup of tea and her bed. She had long since passed the stage of being hungry and wanted to escape only into oblivion.

But here they were met with another check. The worried

landlord met them at the door and unhappily revealed to them that, seeing they were so late in arriving, he had believed he had mistaken the day of their arrival and had let their rooms to another party only half an hour ago.

Chapter 10

IT WAS INDEED the last straw. Lady Danbury began to protest shrilly, and even Lucinda looked slightly daunted. Charles tried manfully to intercede: "But hasn't our baggage arrived yet? We were parted from our train some hours ago, and made sure they would be here before us to warn you we would be coming."

But it appeared that the baggage coaches had not arrived, either, and the landlord had reluctantly given in to the pressure to release the vacant rooms. He was looking extremely apologetic, but could only promise to see what he could do. Perhaps he could manage to convince someone else to willingly give up their rooms—for a price—but what with the gentry flocking abroad these days, demand was extremely high. He could promise nothing.

"Good God, then we'll go somewhere else," snorted Robin, beginning to look like a thundercloud.

But the landlord doubted they would find conditions any better at any of the places they might try, and the three women were appalled at the notion of going back in the rain again to the chilly and uncomfortable carriage. It was finally decided they would wait and see what the landlord might achieve in the way of bribes or threats.

Deveril, surprisingly, had remained quiet until then, but now he said shortly, "Very well. In the meantime, we have yet to dine. That at least you can see to, and at once."

The landlord nearly bowed himself double, looking relieved to be presented with a problem he could so easily solve. He promised to have dinner on the table in half an hour, and when they had eaten he would doubtless have better news for them.

"Aye, you'd better," said Robin with meaning. "At the moment it wouldn't come amiss for me to kick your fat backside for you."

The landlord coldly ignored this ill-bred threat and took himself off again with much repeated bowing. There seemed nothing to do but cool their heels and hope that a place to lay their heads would finally be forthcoming.

Charles, looking much chagrined, said in a low voice to Christina, "My dear, I'm so sorry. The day has been one disaster after another. Will you ever be able to forgive me?"

She was too tired to wish to discuss it, and the headache that had nagged at her earlier had turned into a full-blown pounding behind her eyes. At any rate, it seemed absurd to waste energy in regretting what could not be helped, as Lady Danbury was still doing. Even Lucinda was hanging on Deveril's arm, protesting that she did not mind the wait but looking touchingly exhausted. Christina feared that she herself only managed to look washed out and hag-ridden.

She managed to make some light reply to Charles and changed the subject. But again she could see that he was a little put off by her sangfroid. He said very little during the protracted dinner that followed, but she could only be glad for this unnatural silence. Robin, in the meantime, occupied himself with flirting with Lucinda, so that no one bothered to notice how little Christina ate.

Then unexpectedly Deveril poured out a glass of claret and put it before her, saying curtly, "Here, drink this."

She glanced up and must have shown her astonishment, for he added even more shortly, "It will do you far better than that tea you are maudling your insides with. You look as if you have the headache."

He turned away almost before the words were out, as if it made no difference to him whether she followed his advice or not. And for that reason, and because Charles had roused himself and had begun to look guilty again, she drank the wine without more ado.

And she had to admit that it did help. She could feel it radiating outward, warming the insistent chill deep in her bones, and by the time the landlord bustled back in with several waiters in tow to clear the covers, she was feeling more herself.

At least strong enough not to flinch when the landlord told them, in tones of hearty self-congratulation, that he had good news. He had managed to free three bedchambers that were previously bespoken. He regretted they were not the best in the house, as his lordship had requested, but he hoped they would agree with him that it was better than nothing. And they would be ready as soon as the company had finished dining.

Christina cynically assumed that the landlord had managed to roust three hapless guests from their beds who lacked Deveril's clout. But by that time she was too thankful at the idea of a bed of any kind to cavil at how they were obtained. Still, three bedrooms for six people, none of whom were married, made things more than awkward.

Charles immediately insisted that the three men could share one room, having a truckle bed brought in if necessary, which made Robin look pained. But when it was suggested that Lady

Danbury take one of the remaining bedchambers and Lucinda and Christina share the other, Lucinda blurted, "Oh, but—"

Then she blushed prettily and broke off.

Charles, too, looked torn, and at last said, as if unwillingly, "I fear the thing is, my sister has never been able to stand from a child having anyone else sleep in the room with her. She is a very light sleeper, and it keeps her awake all night."

"No, no, I am sure I am over that by now," Lucinda assured him, not very believably. "I would be delighted to share a room, I promise you, only so long as it has a bed in it. I feel as if I could sleep for a week."

But it was a foregone conclusion that under the circumstances it should be decided that Christina and Lady Danbury share one room and Lucinda take the other.

By that point Christina was past caring, particularly as the landlord was waiting patiently to show them upstairs. But as she glanced around, she chanced on a brief, puzzling interchange between Deveril and the landlord that made her forget her former weariness.

Deveril had been standing, apparently bored, while the prolonged debate had gone on: Lucinda insisting she did not want to make trouble and everyone else arguing that it would be foolish for her to lie awake all night. But as Christina watched, he caught the landlord's eye and gave a microscopic but distinct nod.

The landlord, looking amused, gave the ghost of a wink in return.

For a moment Christina was too tired to do more than take it in in some surprise. Then abruptly she stiffened as the truth hit her, suspicion and sudden rage driving everything else from her head.

There was no thought of holding her tongue or of not confronting Deveril immediately. She could barely contain herself until the others had followed the landlord up the stairs and she was left momentarily alone with him.

"You—*you*!" she cried in a low voice, stumbling over her words a little in her rage. "At last I am beginning to understand. A comedy of disasters? At least Charles was right that it was a comedy, all of your devising, wasn't it, my lord? From the delayed start to the carriage accident, to the misplaced luggage, to the mixup in rooms, it was all your doing! Wasn't it? *Wasn't it?*"

He had continued to look merely bored. "Come, Miss Castleford, I don't know what you're talking about."

"I might have believed that once, but I just saw you exchanging congratulatory smirks with the landlord. Is this how you mean to get even with me? You frightened poor Lady Danbury half to death, put all of us through a miserable day, and all to prove a point to me. My God! They told me you were a devil, but I didn't know the half of it."

"You are imagining things," he drawled. "Either that or becoming hysterical."

She turned abruptly away, knowing she would never make him admit the truth but merely risked losing control completely in front of him. "You are—you are—I have no adjectives left to describe you!" she cried. "Is there no end to what you will dare to get your way?"

"Try me and see," he jeered softly from directly behind her. "I warned you it would be a mistake to underestimate me, Red. Tell me, are you enjoying your trip so far?"

He was gone before she could think of any possible answer to such sheer, monstrous ego.

Nor was there any. She spent the night being forced to acknowledge that bitter and unpalatable truth. She had little doubt now that he had planned everything from the beginning with one object in mind: to make life so miserable for her she would throw up her hands in horror and release what he believed to be her tentacles from Charles. The delayed start, the accident on the road, the inexplicable disappearance of the baggage, and then the giving away of their rooms were obviously all carefully orchestrated. He had even dared to remove Lucinda from any possible danger by suggesting she ride in his phaeton. It was all transparently, monstrously clear now. She need no longer wonder why he had chosen to have the ordering of the journey.

But what kind of monster could coolly plan such a thing, heartlessly involving them all, putting them to inconvenience and distress, to put it no higher? Setting the strings of his amoral mummery going without compunction or any hint of compassion. He was a cold-blooded devil, a—she didn't know any words bad enough to describe him.

And the worst of it was that she could say or do nothing, and he knew it. By keeping that disgraceful episode at the masked ball from Charles, she had seen to it that she must forever remain silent. Were she to tell Charles the truth now, as well as all Deveril's vile threats and insults, he was bound to wonder why she had kept silent for so long. Oh, the devil had been clever. And she, more fool, had played right into his hands.

But even as she thought it, she knew that perhaps the bitterest pill of all was that she had not told Charles the truth for the simple reason that there was some truth to Deveril's accusations. She had been attracted to him. For one moment she had forgotten her cool, practical plans and allowed herself to dream of being swept off her feet by a handsome stranger. Deveril, damn him, had managed to teach her something about herself that she had not suspected or wanted to know: that she was no more immune from the folly of passion and romantic dreams than the next paper-witted woman.

Well, she was cured of that now at least. He was indeed

a devil, and that breathless attraction, that mad kiss in the moonlight, might never have been.

But even there an innate and wholly unwelcome honesty forced her to admit that if she was no longer drawn to him, it was because he had turned off the charm where she was concerned. He despised her now and took no pains to show it. But were he to treat her with that careless, caressing charm and smile at her the way he did Lucinda, it might be different.

And that was another deflating blow. Charles had said Lucinda was shortly to be married, and Christina had begun to wonder after seeing them together that day if it was not Deveril himself she hoped to wed. It would be a natural enough development, after all. Charles and Deveril were old friends, they had all three grown up together, and Lucinda would make Deveril a pretty, conformable wife. Certainly, if her present adoration were anything to go by, she would be unlikely to ask too many awkward questions or curtail his activities when he was out of her company.

Oh, it was all impossible. More than ever marriage to Charles seemed a haven of peace and calm. He would not stir her up or play unspeakable tricks merely to get his own way. He wanted to protect and look after her. She should learn to let him, for what else could a woman desire than to be coddled and cared for, protected from life's every blow? It was what she had dreamed of from a child.

Again she determinedly suppressed her rebellious heart's answer to such a question.

If marriage with Charles were still possible, of course. She had indeed underestimated Deveril's will and ruthlessness. In fact, she did not like to think what he was not capable of in his determination to put a stop to that marriage. If her dead body were discovered on the road to Brussels or drowned in the Channel, she would no longer be in the least surprised.

On that gloomy note she thumped her pillows again, trying to ignore Lady Danbury's snores, and determinedly closed her eyes. Were she to survive the journey it was obvious she would have to stay one jump ahead of Deveril. And that, if today was anything to go by, was unlikely to be either easy or pleasant.

But as she finally drifted off to sleep, it was not of that, or Deveril's perfidy, that her traitorous thoughts insisted upon dwelling. It was the uncharacteristic and inexplicable gesture, given his hatred of her, of his pouring her out a glass of wine to cure her headache. Damn him anyway! He was as annoying and slippery as his namesake, appearing in too many guises to ever quite realize which was the true one. And she would be a fool ever to forget that.

Chapter 11

LUCKILY, the next day passed with no other unpleasantness than the continuing miserable weather. They rose late, the women relieved beyond measure to learn that Deveril's coach had been repaired and was awaiting them below. None of them had relished entering the odoriferous hired vehicle once again. Christina reflected bitterly that such was the power of luxury. They had all quickly come to expect nothing less.

Their missing baggage had also miraculously been restored to them, allowing them the further luxury of a change out of their rumpled garments from the previous day. When asked, Deveril blandly explained that the fools had fallen behind and mistaken the way, then had blundered on for miles on the wrong road before discovering their error.

Christina, with her new knowledge, would have thought no one would believe such nonsense, but everyone seemed to accept it without question. Even Robin seemed uninterested in the reasons for the disappearances, and far more preoccupied with the broken night he had spent on a truckle bed that was far too short for him.

Everyone else seemed fully recovered. Lady Danbury, judging by her snores, had slept extremely well and seemed determined to be in good spirits, and Lucinda emerged from her bedchamber in an extremely becoming traveling dress of palest blue, looking the picture of health and beauty.

Again Christina feared she was letting Charles down, for she knew by comparison she looked pale and listless. It had been very late before she'd fallen asleep, only to be disturbed frequently by her companion, and there were shadows under her eyes and an unbecoming lack of color in her cheeks.

Charles commented on it, saying with touching concern, "My poor love, didn't you sleep? Well, it will be a short day, and tonight will be better. I promise you."

Christina caught Deveril's sardonic eye on them and flushed deeply for some reason. She made some mild reply to Charles, assuring him she had slept perfectly, all the while reflecting bitterly that Deveril, curse him, was indeed managing to come between them. With his mocking eyes on her she seemed unable to behave naturally in Charles's presence, which Charles certainly must soon be able to detect. Robin's bet with himself came back to haunt her, and the journey began to take on an even more nightmarish quality. She must end this unnatural obsession with Deveril before she achieved what he could not, for all his scheming—a rift between her and Charles.

She therefore deliberately turned her back on Deveril and ignored him for the rest of the day. She did not visibly snub him, and answered any questions he might put to her. But she avoided any opportunity to be alone with him and never willingly looked in his direction again. If she was aware of his unpleasant silver eyes on her frequently, as if probing for a weak spot, she refused to give him the satisfaction of showing it.

She had dreaded encountering more "mishaps," but they arrived at Dover by early afternoon without further trouble. The continued rain had affected everyone's spirits to a certain extent, even Lucinda's, but on the surface at least they were still a pleasant party traveling together for pleasure.

The elegant hotel had not misplaced their rooms, Deveril's agent was discovered waiting for them with comfortable news of his lordship's yacht and crew, and everyone else in the party breathed a sigh of relief, thinking things had returned to normal. Christina merely waited for the next blow to fall.

It did in the shape of continued rain, but surely even Deveril could not be responsible for that. For several days they were obliged to cool their heels, waiting for the weather to improve and Deveril's captain, a bluff, good-natured man, to pronounce the winds favorable for the crossing.

Christina remained indoors, tied by the heels to Lady Danbury, who refused to set foot outside in such weather. But Lucinda went out several times for short drives with Deveril, returning damp and laughing, evidently on the best of terms with him. It was obvious he did not live up to his nickname in her presence, for she positively glowed when he was around.

Robin escaped several times as well, though probably on less harmless excursions. He was growing bored with such a family party and half regretting he had come. As the days of rain wore on, Christina would not have been surprised to discover he had changed his mind and meant to abandon them, for his moods were always mercurial and he was used to very different entertainment than playing whist with Lady Danbury or flirting mildly with Lucinda under her brother's eye.

But though he complained loudly in his sister's presence, he remained with the party. When Christina once asked him bluntly why he stayed when he was so plainly bored, he merely shrugged and gave her one of his mischievous grins. "Curiosity," he admitted frankly. "Your worthy fiancé may be likable, my pet, but he's deucedly blind, as are the rest of this ill-assorted party. Or did you hope I was too?'' he added mockingly.

She flushed, for it was a subject she had no desire to discuss with him. In her first hot fury she had been strongly tempted to confide in Robin, but by morning wiser thoughts had prevailed. There was never any predicting how Robin would take something. He might himself, still chafing under a miserable day and night, have been furious and challenged Deveril with it on the spot, which would have undone everything. Or he might merely have been amused. Either way, it would only make an impossible situation worse, and she could certainly do without adding Robin's knowing eyes to those already watching her. He was entirely too shrewd sometimes.

"Besides," Robin added, grinning, "I have my own reasons for going, don't forget."

Christina had indeed momentarily forgotten that mysterious packet, and wished she had not been reminded of it now. She had tackled him with it again during the long delay, but could get nothing more out of him than that it was a private spot of business. Until she married Charles and the dibs were in tune again, he would have to make do the best he could.

She told herself that Robin was just being mysterious, as he loved to be. But the reminder did nothing to add to her peace of mind.

But trouble, when it next came, was from a wholly unexpected quarter. Lady Danbury had already proved a somewhat inconvenient traveling companion, but it soon developed that she was a very bad sailor, and her notion of calm seas and Deveril's captain's were very different. On the third day they woke to gray but clear skies, and Captain Ramey pronounced the tide favorable. But Lady Danbury took one look at the angrily tossing seas and refused to set foot on board his lordship's yacht.

Charles did his best to persuade her, and even Robin, for he had long since grown bored with the lack of entertainment. But Lady Danbury remained adamant. They might go without her, but they would not get her on board, not so long as the weather continued like this. She had once taken a day's sailing to Jersey on what they had promised her was mild seas, and nearly died of seasickness. She hated to be disobliging, but not even for their sakes would she risk her health again.

There seemed nothing for it but to wait for calmer seas. Christina was at least thankful to finally be able to escape outdoors, and took a long walk with Charles along the cliffs. She returned windblown and red with the cold, but for a few hours she had managed to forget everything and had enjoyed herself immensely.

Charles had proven his usual charming self. He had feared to exhaust her and repeatedly asked if she didn't want to return, which was a nuisance since she was no hothouse flower. But he was touchingly happy to get her to himself for once. "I thought this journey was a good idea," he admitted, smiling. "But now I'm beginning to wonder. However fond I may be of my sister and your brother—and Deveril, of course—they're always underfoot. I am beginning to feel a little as one does at a house party when you are weathered in: confoundedly constricted and tired of seeing the same faces day after day."

Then he carried her hand to his lips and added, "But it will soon pass, I know. I keep reminding myself that in a few weeks you will be my wife. It hardly seems real, doesn't it?"

Christina was a little startled to discover the truth of his words. Their marriage did seem unreal now, like some forgotten dream. Where before the mere mention of it would have conjured up a warm glow in her, as if she would be safe and happy at last, now she felt nothing more than a vague disquiet.

She instantly dismissed the traitorous notion, blaming it on Deveril and the uncertainty he had created. But still, she was a little disquieted to discover that marriage to Charles had somehow ceased to represent the serenity it once had done.

Then she realized she was once more allowing Deveril to come between her and Charles, even if only in thought, and determinedly put him out of her mind. She would not let him ruin everything for her. She would not.

But when they returned at the end of a happy hour or two Deveril was coming down the stairs, as if waiting for them. He took in Christina's red cheeks and tousled hair, his eyes unreadable, and she instantly flushed even more, despising herself for caring how she looked in his presence.

But Charles hailed him laughingly. "There you are, you layabout. We have been walking along the cliffs. Christina is intrepid. I feared to exhaust her long ago, but she assures me she's a country girl, used to tramping for miles."

Deveril's brows rose politely. "Oh? You are to be congratulated, Miss Castleford, for your joy in such . . . earthy pleasures."

Charles frowned, perhaps seeing her in a new light, as Deveril certainly had intended. But he quickly dismissed the traitorous thought. "Yes, I told you she was unusual, didn't I? She will make me an excellent wife, you must admit. Few other women would be eager for such exercise, or so uncomplaining about the mud I have just tracked in." Again he squeezed Christina's hand warmly.

Deveril eyed their linked hands, and his expression was at its most unpleasant. "You are indeed to be congratulated," he said, and left it at that.

Christina went upstairs in a fit of temper and ruthlessly restored her bright hair to its usual sedate state, then changed her damp dress. It was impossible! Everywhere she went, he was there, with his malicious silver eyes and his disapproval. He was almost the first one she saw in the morning, and the last one at night. He had taken to mockingly handing her her bedroom candle when she retired, and bidding her a polite good night. His hated eyes had even begun to haunt her dreams.

For a moment wild thoughts possessed her of throwing it all over and making Robin take her back to London. But to what? she realistically reminded herself. Grandmama's disapproval and sale to the highest bidder? She had long ago cold-heartedly realized that marriage was the only escape for her, and marriage to Charles, with his quick, warm smile and kind concern, had seemed far preferable to one of her grandmama's handpicked wealthy and unpleasant candidates.

But perhaps even that was preferable to fighting Deveril. He had assured her he would blink at nothing to defeat her, and she was beginning to believe that he was right. There was no move she could make he would not counter—no way to escape him.

Then she was annoyed at herself. However much he liked to believe himself unbeatable, he was but a man, after all, not the devil he sometimes seemed. She was a fool to let him begin to haunt her like this, investing him with seemingly superhuman traits.

Luckily, on the fifth day the weather dawned sunny and perfect, and even Lady Danbury was at last convinced by the combined efforts of the captain, Charles, and Christina that the Channel was unlikely to get much calmer. She at last reluctantly consented to sail the next morning, provided conditions did not deteriorate overnight.

It was obvious she strongly suspected they would do so, but in this she was proved wrong. They rose early on the sixth morning to the reassurance from the captain that it was going to be another fine day. With any luck they would be in France by seven that evening. Deveril's agent had gone over days before to make the necessary arrangements, and had probably long since begun to wonder what had happened to them.

Lady Danbury balked again a little at the thought of some twelve hours at sea, but by dint of much persuasion from Charles and Robin, she at last gave way. The morning was indeed fresh and beautiful, with a brisk wind and the now familiar smell of salt in the air. Deveril's yacht had also become a familiar sight, for it had been visible from the windows of the inn, looking incredibly graceful and disdainful as much uglier vessels had come and departed over the days they had waited.

Christina had found the port fascinating and had spent some hours standing and watching the activity. While they had cooled their heels, a dozen ships had arrived and gone, from the daily packets to Calais and Ostend, to trading ships, to one or two graceful yachts like *Devil's Lady.*

It was something of a minor victory to all of them when Lady Danbury at last consented to step aboard, and though she immediately went below to her cabin, Christina remained above watching as the baggage was loaded. Deveril had gone to confer with his captain, Lucinda and Robin were curiously exploring the ship, and Charles had gone to see that Lady Danbury was comfortable.

Christina watched curiously as a huge net was hoisted, containing the last of the baggage and several miscellaneous boxes, and swung over toward the yacht. Some fresh-faced young seamen were waiting to receive it and stow it below, eager no doubt to be away from port.

But even as she watched, something seemed to go wrong. The huge hook holding the net jerked and seemed to stick: the net seemed to have been imperfectly fixed, for the next thing she knew, it had given way, and the baggage and supplies tumbled straight into the oily waters of the Channel.

With an almost resigned feeling of déjà vu Christina recognized her own portmanteaux before they disappeared beneath the water forever.

Chapter 12

THE CAPTAIN was most apologetic, Charles aghast, and Robin inclined to be furious at this newest mishap. Once the extent of it became known, he stormed up and down the deck, demanding that something be done immediately and whoever was responsible dismissed for such criminal carelessness.

Deveril intervened at last. "Unfortunately, nothing can be done," he said coldly. "Your sister's things are already at the bottom of the Channel. I will, naturally, recompense her for any damage she suffered."

"No, no. Of course it is not your fault," interjected Charles. "That would be my responsibility."

"Aye, that's all very well! But what's she to do in the meantime?" demanded Robin, still in high dudgeon. "She can't jaunt all the way to Brussels in the clothes she stands up in."

"I can lend her whatever she may need," Lucinda offered, evidently alarmed at the threat of further delays. "We're about the same size."

They had put off sailing, at risk of missing the tide, while it was decided what to do in the wake of this latest disaster. Robin was all for returning ashore immediately, but as Charles pointed out reasonably, Christina might as easily replace what was needed urgently on the French as well as the English side of the Channel.

Christina, after one livid look, had not glanced again at Deveril, afraid to see the secret amusement in his eyes. She had remained silent during this debate, cursing Deveril as much for making her the object of pity and attention as for the loss of her trunks. Nor had she any intention of giving him the satisfaction of knowing that his sabotage had succeeded far better this time than any of the others. Virtually everything she owned had just disappeared into the sea, and last-minute expenses had been such that her pockets were almost wholly to let.

At last she spoke up wearily, "It doesn't matter. Pray let us drop the subject and go on."

She was rewarded by one of Charles's warm smiles. "Yes, let us go on. We have come too far to turn back now. At any rate, it will give me the excuse to buy my bride an entire new wardrobe," he joked. "She has been so stubborn she has scarcely let me give her a thing."

This time Christina could feel the weight of Deveril's skeptical silver gaze on her, but refused to give it acknowledgment in any way. She had indeed refused to let Charles give her anything more than trinkets until now— though Deveril clearly didn't believe it. It had been a measure of foolish pride perhaps, but it had been important to her. Now to be placed in the position of allowing him to buy even her bride clothes was untenable.

Unfortunately, it seemed she had little choice. What money she had brought with her had been tucked into one of her trunks for safekeeping—an added irony. She had scarcely enough left to replace even her barest necessities, let alone an entire wardrobe.

Nor was Robin likely to be able to help, for he was always under the hatches. To be reduced to borrowing from Lucinda, or allow Charles to purchase the very shifts she wore, was intolerably humiliating.

Oh, yes, if Deveril's object had been to make things unpleasant for her, he had certainly succeeded. She would have wept with vexation—or, far more preferable, cursed and swore at him—if it would have done any good. But both would merely give him a satisfaction she had no intention of allowing him.

The fourth option, that he would indeed replace her wardrobe as he said, did not even occur to her. He had done it to humiliate her, he had succeeded, and he would be the last one to lessen that humiliation.

Under the circumstances, the charm of being at sea for the first time was wasted on her. Lucinda hung on Deveril's arm, looking enchantingly pretty with her cheeks snapping with cold and her eyes excited. She demanded to be told the name of everything and seemed delighted with the experience, insisting again and again that she never dreamed sailing could be so exciting.

As usual, Deveril behaved toward her with an uncharacteristic indulgence. He patiently answered all her questions, showed her around, and once caught her when she nearly slipped. He held her for a moment, laughing down at her, looking very different from his usual sardonic self and showing a side of himself that Christina had never seen.

Or, she reminded herself with an odd pang, she had seen it once. That first magical night at the ball.

But it did no good to remember that, for it was the source of all her present troubles. No more good than to realize that under other circumstances she would have longed to be shown over the graceful yacht herself. But Deveril would now never turn that indulgent smile on her, or treat her with the amused tolerance he was showing Lucinda. He was her enemy, and she had better remember it.

On that thought she went below to check on Lady Danbury, telling herself it was duty and not the unpleasant sight of Deveril doting on Lucinda that drove her. She only knew that she was finding oddly little pleasure in her first trip out of England, or her first sea voyage.

She found Lady Danbury in a sad state. She herself had felt only a mild awareness of the tossing of the yacht, but then her mind had had a great deal more on it than her physical well-being. But Lady Danbury had already turned a mild shade of green and had retired to her bed.

Her maid was in attendance, but Lady Danbury exclaimed at Christina's coming as at a lifeline. And since the maid herself was looking decidedly unwell and had to quickly excuse herself, Christina was thankfully kept busy for the next several hours.

Lady Danbury's discomfort grew steadily worse. It was a hard illness for an outsider to comprehend, especially since Christina herself felt no twinge and was evidently a born sailor. But she had to acknowledge that her patient's suffering was very real. Lady Danbury retched endlessly until nothing more remained on her stomach, and she was finally reduced to moaning on her bed and begging to be allowed to die in peace.

There had been no further sign of the maid, from which Christina deduced that she was similarly afflicted. Once, when she went out to fetch some fresh water, she discovered from one of the stewards that Lucinda, despite her earlier bravado, had retired to her cabin and was feeling far from well. But since he also reported she had her maid with her, Christina felt no necessity to go and check on her.

The seaman also informed her, with a grin, that they were coming on a squall, and happen the rest of the passengers would be suffering the same fate soon enough. "Except for his lordship, o' course. He can ride out a typhoon without feeling the effects of it. Are you sure you're all right, miss?''

"Yes, quite all right, thank you," Christina was able to inform him truthfully. "But poor Lady Danbury is very miserable, I fear. What is the best thing to do for her, do you know?''

The seaman grinned again, with the cheerful contempt that sailors feel for the less hardy, and allowed as how the only thing he knew to cure seasickness was dry land. That or a healthy dram that allowed the sufferer to sleep it off.

"Oh, yes!" Christina seized on that gratefully. "I don't know why I didn't think of that sooner myself. Can you fetch me some brandy?''

The seaman did so willingly and promised to look in again in a half hour or so to see if she needed anything else. But Lady Danbury merely moaned at the sight of the tumbler, and requested Christina in a voice of loathing to go away and leave her to die.

"Yes, dearest ma'am, I will, as soon as you've drunk this. One of the sailors assures me it is the only thing to help. It will put you to sleep, you know, which will be the very best thing, I promise you.''

Lady Danbury at last agreed weakly to drink it, as much, Christina suspected, to put an end to the argument as because she really thought it would help. But in the end it did manage to put her to sleep, which was a decided improvement.

For another hour Christina sat in the stuffy room, afraid to leave her in case she should waken, and even afraid to open the window, since she had objected strongly before to such a suggestion.

But at last her continued heavy slumber and the increasingly unpleasant air in the cabin at last drove her out and up on deck for a brief breath of much needed fresh air.

She found that it had grown quite dark, though it could only be early afternoon, and that the deck was empty. The wind had picked up considerably, and it looked as if they were indeed in for a squall, as the sailor had warned her.

Christina's cloak billowed out with the wind, and her hair began to come loose from its pins, but she found the experience oddly exhilarating. It seemed to her they were going at an enormous speed, and since the wind and the waves drowned out any other sound, it seemed she was the only one alive in the elements.

A sailor soon came by to shatter that illusion. But when asked, he agreed more sedately than her earlier acquaintance that they were indeed in for a rough time of it. "Happen you should go below, miss, with the rest of 'em."

"Why, are they all seasick?" asked Christina, startled.

But the sailor could venture no answer to that. Miss Heybridge was feeling a mite under the weather, so he was led to understand, and Mr. Heybridge had repaired to his own cabin, himself complaining of considerable discomfort. As for her ladyship's maid and the gentleman's man, they was both sick as dogs, if the belowdecks steward was to be believed.

Only Robin, it seemed, had escaped the general malaise, but he too had gone below, apparently finding himself bored by the lack of company. As for his lordship, "No, bless you, miss, he don't suffer from seasickness," the seaman said in amusement. "A born sailor is his lordship." But it seemed he was in conference with the captain about their proposed route, since it looked like they were in for a bit of a blow.

Christina couldn't help laughing a little to think of them all laid low by seasickness, although it was undoubtedly unkind. She herself had never felt more alive, and since it seemed she was to have the deck to herself, she could remain above for a little longer. She had no desire at all to run into Deveril, which seemed her only danger. But he was safely occupied elsewhere for the time being.

She stood there uninterrupted for more than an hour, clinging to the railing, feeling the wind lift her hair completely from its careful coils and throw the salt water in her face. The wind was almost a tangible presence, so strong she had to lean into it, and it filled the sails above with a cracking thunder that drove them across the seas.

She knew she should go below, for she feared she was making a spectacle of herself, wet and untidy, laughing into the wind like some ancient pagan worshipper. But no one came to disturb her, and she felt uplifted and unlike herself. There was nothing in the world but the water and the wind, both awesome forces of nature, and it was easy to see why earlier ages had respected and feared them.

As unkind fate would have it, however, it was finally Deveril who came to destroy her newfound freedom. "So you take to sailing, do you?" he inquired mockingly from behind her. "I should have known you would."

The way he said it was no compliment, and she turned on him instantly, furious to be discovered in so revealing a moment and uncomfortably aware of her bedraggled appearance.

"I was just going below," she said coldly, and made to pass him.

He barred her way as he had done long ago. "No you weren't," he said in amusement, taking in her wind-tangled hair and betraying color. "You were out here reveling in the elements like the little pagan you are."

It was so akin to her own earlier thoughts that she must have gaped at him, for he added, "Why do you look so surprised? I told you we were much alike, didn't I? Why do you think I bought the *Devil's Lady*?"

Again she was surprised, but she thought this conversation had gone on long enough, so she pushed past him without comment.

But his next words stopped her. "Don't you have something to say to me? Aren't you going to berate me for the loss of your baggage?"

He still sounded mockingly amused, and for a moment his effrontery almost overcame her. But she still had no intention of giving him any more satisfaction, and so said shortly, "Would it do any good if I did?"

"None in the least," he admitted cheerfully. "Are you ready to admit you're defeated?"

"Go to hell!" she said, and started again toward the companionway.

He laughed and caught her wrist, physically preventing her. "I will, if I can take you with me. Believe me, Red, you are wasted on Charles. Haven't you yet discovered that he likes his women fragile and helpless? You are about as helpless as a black widow spider."

It was too near the truth, and she reacted instinctively. "I told you not to call me that!" she cried furiously. "And let go of me. I am going below."

He held her easily. "I regret such fine disdain is wasted at the moment, my dear, since you look like a half-drowned rat."

"You—you—!" She could not think of any words bad enough.

This time he laughed, a great, soaring release. "No, I am just being unkind. You look, in truth, like some sea witch with your red hair blowing about your face and your eyes full of excitement. Why the devil are you wasting your efforts on Charles, you little fool? You might have gone after much bigger game."

"Like you, for instance?" she demanded contemptuously. He still held her by the wrist, but she had ceased struggling, deeming it undignified.

But he refused to rise to the bait. "I will admit, inspired

by the moment and between us only, that you have managed to surprise me this last week. I always knew you were beautiful enough to captivate any man. But I will concede you are magnificent. I begin to understand your grandmother's phenomenal success. Only take your talons out of Charles and I will become your greatest admirer. Refuse, and I think you already see what I am capable of.''

''You mean I am magnificent in the role you have designed for me,'' she said scornfully. When he merely nodded carelessly, she had to control her voice before she could speak again. ''And did it never occur to you that I might love Charles?''

He added to her fury by grinning insultingly. ''No. I have watched you in close company together for more than a week now, and you are no more in love with Charles than you are with me. Which leaves only one thing you want from him, doesn't it?''

Without thinking, she raised her other arm and slapped him as hard as she could across his mocking, devil's face.

Chapter 13

FOR A MOMENT the violence shocked both of them. Christina was secretly appalled, for she had never in her life struck another human being in anger. For his part, Deveril looked first stunned, and then all expression was wiped from his face as the imprint of her hand showed white, then darkly red against his lean cheek.

His grip on her wrist tightened cruelly, however, and Christina knew in that moment that she was deathly afraid of him. The wild elements of the storm and violence seemed to become one, and her earlier thought of murder no longer seemed so farfetched. Were he to force her overboard—and it was highly doubtful that she could prevent him if he chose to—no one would ever suspect anything but a tragic accident.

In fact, he need merely pick her up in those powerful arms and drop her into the churning, angry sea, and her screams would go unheard, snatched away on the fierce wind. Long before the icy water closed over her head for the last time *Devil's Lady* would be far away, unable to save her.

The image was so real that when he abruptly jerked her against him she struggled with a pent-up strength she had not known she possessed. The storm and her own fear all seemed to inextricably combine as he ruthlessly tried to bend her to his will, careless of how he might hurt her.

His hard hands bruised her, but that fact sank to insignificance in the face of the dark purpose she saw in his lean face so close to her own. He seemed indeed a devil to her in that moment as he silently sought to control both of her hands and force them behind her back.

For herself, she was beyond all considerations of modesty by then, and fought back with an animal's weapons, teeth and fingernails. She knew she was struggling for survival, and she was beyond rational thought or emotion. The only reality was his hard hands and body, inch by inch gaining ascendency and subduing her to his will, and the screaming wind that threw her hair in her face to blind her and that snatched her desperate cries even from her own ears.

Then he had thrust both her hands behind her back, holding them cruelly and forcing her up against him, and he was shouting in her ear against the wind, "You little fool! Be still, damn you!"

The rest of his words were lost to her, snatched away in the wind, and she ignored them, knowing that weakness meant her death. Were she to give into him she would be lost, and Deveril would succeed in claiming her forever. It made no sense, for he would be alive and she dead, but then he was the devil, and he could do anything. Even make her desire to stop fighting him and give in to the inevitability of her own death.

With that thought she roused herself to renewed effort, struggling violently against him even though she knew it was no use. He had said he would stop at nothing to keep her from marrying Charles, and this would be the surest method of preventing her. But she was weak, and he was so strong, so strong. Whatever she did his hands gained mastery, and his hard body held her, dominated her, forcing her to give in to him against her will.

She knew her terror and panic must now be transparent in her face and eyes, but that no longer mattered either.

Then Deveril swore, violently and profanely, as he caught a glimpse of her face and seemed to redouble his efforts, as if he had only been playing with her before. He forced her up against the rail, one hand holding her arms immobile and the other bending her inexorably back across his arm so that she was leaning periously over the rail. She could feel the wet spray now, as if the Channel were already reaching out to her, and her hair blew wildly, extended out on the gale like the flame of a torch.

He was winning. Soon he would pick up her legs, and she would be falling, falling, grasping uselessly at the air and screaming, until the water closed over her head and filled up her mouth and nose and her scream choked in her throat. And through it all he would stand there, laughing with those silvery eyes of his, while she fought the water for a brief time, buoyed up by her cloak, until it, too, grew waterlogged and pulled her down for the last time.

She closed her eyes and the images seemed so real before her tightly closed lids that it took her a moment or two to realize that the struggle had changed. He still held her forced over the railing, her hands caught behind her back and her body immobile, but he seemed content merely to subdue her and made no move to bundle her over the rail into the sea.

Then he said loudly, against the snatch of the wind, "Sweet Christ! Did you really think I meant to murder you, you little fool?"

Her eyes opened slowly to see the mockery in his silver ones—and something else far less easy to read and which might almost have been anger. The slowly receding panic in her own must have been far easier to decipher, for he swore again briefly and then roughly pulled her up, away from the rail and the sea below, and then released her.

It was so sudden, and she had gone so far down the road to envisioning her own end that for a moment she was dizzy. She was forced to cling to him, where before she had fought in panic to be free. At first he was rigid under her grasp. Then with a violent exclamation he pulled her into his arms and held her, his hand in her streaming hair holding her head tightly pressed against his chest as if he would never let her go.

And it was as much a part of the madness of the storm, both within and without her, that she could now take comfort from the man she had thought her murderer. She clung to him, refusing for the moment to return to the hard demands of reality, oddly content to feel only the strong beat of his heart under her ear and the amazing tremor caused by his lips in her tangled hair.

Then a wave driven by the increasing gale crashed overboard and drenched them, and reality returned with a vengeance. She gasped and stiffened, but before she could pull away, Deveril had dragged them both to shelter against the deck house.

They were both wet and cold by then, their hair streaming and their garments sodden. Certainly any earlier madness should have been forgotten in the reality of cold discomfort. But with a strange sound that was half exclamation, half smothered laugh, Deveril tightened his grip upon her, taking in her bedraggled appearance. "God, Red, I think you are a witch," he said.

And then he was kissing her with some of the earlier violence that had flared between them, and Christina fatalistically knew again the feeling of drowning that she had just so vividly envisioned.

How long it would have gone on, or who would have

roused first to more practical considerations, neither of them knew. It took another wave, larger than the last, to bring them belatedly to their senses. Deveril gave another laugh, less smothered this time, and said regretfully, "Enjoyable as this is, sweetheart, I think we had better go below before we are both drowned. Or do you still think that's part of my devilish plot?"

His words and the dash of cold water were enough, where they should have been before, to bring her to her shocked senses at last. She was aghast at her behavior, and without another word she pulled herself from his arms and struggled to the companionway.

It was even more humiliating to have to wait for his help to open the door in the face of the wind, before she could negotiate the narrow stairs to the cabins below. She did so, her wet cloak clinging unpleasantly to her and her hair streaming with water, dreading to meet someone and dreading even more to hear one of Deveril's devastating comments, this time so richly deserved.

But fortunately they met no one, and at the door of her cabin he merely opened it for her and said rather roughly, "Go in and get out of those wet things. I'll send someone with a change of clothes for you. And don't go above again while the storm lasts."

She had time to notice that he looked very different from the usual elegant Lord Deveril. His black hair was also streaming and hung across his forehead in becoming disarray; his coat and shirt were wet and clinging, his cravat ruined. But more, he looked younger than she had ever seen him before, more carefree, less the cynical devil she knew. "You know this isn't finished between us, don't you?" he demanded arrogantly, as a threat. "There is still a reckoning for us, and I won't wait much longer. So be warned."

When he was gone Christina was left to face not only the ruin of her one remaining dress, but the far more devastating ashes of her pride and the undreamed-of magnitude of her own folly.

They landed at Ostend without further mishap. True to his word, Deveril had sent a servant with a change of clothes, but whether they were Lucinda's or not Christina was never to discover. Certainly no one showed any inclination, when they at last met again on deck, to ask what she had been doing during the long hours at sea. They all seemed to assume that, like them, she had spent the time battling *mal de mer*, not a far more elemental and dangerous struggle.

Lady Danbury had revived enough at the thought of land, when Christina at last went to her, to totter out of her bed and make it above deck under her own power. Her maid, too, seemed to have recovered from her brief illness and returned to her duties with many apologies.

Lucinda was looking a trifle pale, but swore she had not been sick, just slightly queasy. Charles laughed at this patent falsehood and confessed readily that he himself had been as sick as a dog. "I don't know what it is. I never go to sea without vowing to myself no one will ever drag me there again. Then, sure enough, by the time the next journey is suggested, enough time has passed that I have managed to forget my misery. By contrast Blaise, the devil, never feels a twinge. Do you, old friend?"

Deveril was engaged in low conversation with his captain, but he looked around at that and answered rather absently, "No, I have a strong stomach." Then he glanced up and his eyes seemed to locate Christina, for he added, as if deliberately, "You missed a splendid storm, you know."

Charles groaned. "Do you see what I mean?" he said,

appealing to his betrothed. "No sensibilities whatsoever. How about you? I hope you at least managed to get some sleep."

She made some noncommittal answer, eager to be on shore and away from Deveril's piercing silver eyes. The thought of the rest of the journey in his company had now become impossible, and she was strongly tempted to abandon everything and beg, borrow, or steal her passage back to England.

But Charles remained blessedly normal, seemingly a rock to cling to in her present confusion. If he thought her abnormally quiet, he obviously laid it down to the difficulties of the crossing, and was touchingly solicitous of her wellbeing on the short trip to the inn Deveril's agent had booked for them. Still aware of Deveril's eyes on her, no doubt filled with contemptuous mockery, Christina clung to Charles as to a lifeline.

She pleaded tiredness as an excuse to skip dinner and go straight to bed, and since the rest of the ladies were in the same state, this request raised none but perhaps Deveril's eyebrows. But she didn't look to find out.

Robin had claimed to have slept through the storm unscathed, but he, too, seemed slightly subdued since they had reached the Continent. After the gentlemen had retired for the night he came and knocked on his sister's bedchamber door, ostensibly to check that she was all right but in reality, Christina suspected, because he wanted to talk.

He was relieved to find her still awake, though attired in the nightrobe and wrapper Lucinda had leant her. "Very fetching." He grinned, taking in the somewhat extravagant lace on these garments. "And at least now you have no further excuse to quibble over Charles buying you a trousseau. I only wish you'd done so before you sank a fortune in clothes. It would have saved me a lot of trouble."

Christina turned away from the door and climbed back into

bed, cold to her soul and in no mood for Robin's notion of humor. "Oh, go away, Robin," she said wearily. "I need to get some rest."

He had gone to turn over her brushes and combs on the dressing table, but now he turned to regard her rather searchingly. "Yes, you don't look well," he said surprisingly. "Did you manage to get any sleep on the crossing?"

Instantly she was alert, though she told herself it was merely her guilty conscience. Robin could know nothing. "I managed to get a little sleep, but I spent most of the time with Lady Danbury. Why do you ask?"

"Oh, no reason." Robin was elaborately casual, which further increased her suspicions. "I just wondered. By the way, how is my wager doing?"

"Your wager?"

"Surely you can't have forgotten. I had a wager with myself about how long it would take the estimable Charles to tumble to the enmity between you and Deveril. Has he yet? I must admit I see no signs of it."

"Oh, go to bed," she said again.

"Well, sleep tight," he said lightly. "I just wondered— you do still mean to wed Charles, don't you? You haven't changed your mind about that?"

She started, fearing he knew something, but it was always impossible to read his thoughts. "No, I haven't changed my mind," she said at last.

But when he had gone she wondered if it was true—and why Robin should suddenly be so anxious to know. Both prevented her from getting the sleep she had said she so badly needed.

Oddly enough, the question was repeated the next morning from a far more formidable source. Christina had delayed going downstairs until the last moment, desiring a tête-à-tête with no one. She emerged from the inn just as the baggage was being loaded on the familiar coach with Deveril's crest on the panels.

That stopped her for a moment. Charles, seeing her astonishment, said in amusement, "Deveril had it shipped over. Can you believe it? What it must be to be rich. I fear you may begin to regret your betrothal to me in the face of all this luxury."

"Never!" she snapped, unable to understand why the ostentatious gesture should so enrage her. "I think it's ridiculous."

"I'm glad, but Lucinda doesn't, I'm afraid. I only hope—" Then he stopped himself and flushed. "Never mind."

She suddenly had to know, though she acknowledged now the answer would cause her pain. "You only hope she won't be disappointed," she finished for him calmly. "You said once that you expected her to marry shortly. I take it it was Deveril you had in mind?"

He turned to her a little eagerly. "Yes. I admit it. He—well, I'm sure you know he has something of the reputation of a rake. But it is largely undeserved, I assure you. And that ridiculous nickname infuriates me. You know they call him the Devil. But he has been a good friend to me, and he's devilish fond of Lucinda. You saw the pains he's taken over this trip. I suspect that was as much for her benefit as mine. All I know is, she's confident he means to propose when we get to Brussels. I agree with her, and confess I will welcome it. Just think. We will all be related more closely than mere friends."

Christina could only once again marvel at his blindness, but she was aware of a bitter taste at the back of her mouth as well. Would Charles—and Lucinda—be so eager for such a marriage if they knew Deveril was kissing her only last night? Or, like Deveril, would they merely put it down to the nature of the male sex, to whom such escapades obviously meant nothing?

Christina was hoping to avoid Deveril that morning, but to her chagrin he managed to corner her while Charles went to fetch something for Lady Danbury, who was still mislaying things.

There was a pleasant smile on his lips, no doubt for the others' benefit, but his silvery eyes were uncomfortably fixed on her face. "So," he said sardonically, "you still mean to marry Charles even after last night? You have been hanging on his arm for the last twelve hours as if your life depended on it."

She thought perhaps it might, but made herself lift her chin and defiantly confront him. "Yes," she said deliberately. "Is there any reason why I shouldn't?"

He laughed harshly. "If you don't know the answer to that one, Red, I'm not going to tell you. I am only sorry for Charles, poor devil. He didn't stand a chance against you. Even I, knowing what you are, was almost fooled."

His words stung, as they were meant to. Wanting to wound him back, she said the first thing that entered her head: "This is nonsense. When you are married to Lucinda and I to Charles, we will have to meet without being at daggers drawn. It is foolish for us to go on quarreling."

"You needn't worry, Miss Castleford," he said, his eyes insulting. "The day you are wed to Charles will be the day I cease to cross his threshold, believe me. Nor shall I be the only one. But why should that bother you? You will have gotten what you want, though you will have ruined Charles in the process." He strode away without another word.

She stared bleakly after him, telling herself he had said nothing he hadn't said before and in far stronger terms. But it wasn't true. There was very little he hadn't said to her

before, by way of insult, but there had always been an under-
tone of amusement in it, as if he took very little of it seriously.
Despite herself she had almost believed that he meant it when
he said were she to remove her hold on Charles he would
be her greatest admirer.

But he had never looked at her as if he hated her before,
as he had just done, or said such biting, wounding things.
She told herself bravely it was mere pique, for she knew well
he didn't like not getting his way.

But still she could not help wondering why she felt so
shaken, as if she were in the wrong this time, not him.

Chapter 14

AFTER THAT Christina took more care to avoid Deveril. He had had his curricle and pair shipped over, as well as Robin's and Charles's mounts, so they set out at an early hour in their familiar pattern. For once they suffered no more serious mishap than Charles discovering the bruises on Christina's arms at the first stop.

"Good God," he said, taking one of her arms and examining the deep bruising around her wrist and forearm. "How on earth did that happen?"

Christina flushed guiltily, furious with herself for having allowed her sleeve to fall back. She had discovered the bruises herself the night before and had quickly covered them up again, not liking to be reminded of those moments of insanity in the storm. Certainly she had not wanted to invite any questions about the marks.

She managed to make some answer about having stumbled in her cabin during the storm and it seemed to satisfy Charles, but she was deeply aware as she did so of Deveril's arrested attention behind them.

"You should take more care, Miss Castleford," he said harshly. "It would appear you are oddly accident prone."

Her eyes flashed involuntarily to his with a message of

contempt to match his own. "I intend to," she said, and left it at that.

Charles looked a little puzzled at this exchange, but seemed to put it down to Deveril's bad mood. His lordship had addressed few remarks to anyone that morning, and there was a bleak look on his face that did not invite conversation. Even Lucinda had suffered a rebuff, for she had begged prettily to be allowed to drive with him again and been curtly refused.

Christina did not flatter herself his temper had anything to do with her—unless, of course, he really had confidently expected her to fall at his feet after no more than a few kisses. But it effectively cast a damper on the rest of the party, especially after the difficult crossing. Lady Danbury dozed most of the day, Robin remained in an odd, jumpy humor, and Lucinda tended to sulk. She bothered to arouse herself only at the brief stops to change horses, when she sprang to sparkling life. She seemed to be intent on ignoring Deveril's mood and drawing him out. Christina almost felt sorry for her.

She herself was content merely to remain out of his way. And in that Deveril seemed to be abetting her, for that brief unpleasant exchange was the only one that passed between them all day.

Charles was once more the passenger in his curricle, and they seldom bothered to remain behind with the slower-moving coaches. Deveril, in fact, seemed to be taking his bad temper out on his horses, for at the first stop they were seen to be heavily lathered and nearly exhausted.

By the second stop he seemed to have gotten his temper under control, and he at least made an effort to be civil to the others. But he did not once glance again in Christina's direction or speak to her.

She told herself fiercely that she was glad. In twenty-four

hours they would be in Brussels and free of the enforced intimacy of traveling together. After that they would meet only publicly, and that as little as she could contrive. Unless he meant to betray her at this late date, which seemed unlikely, she supposed they would of necessity manage to be polite to one another in public. But it was obvious it would be a strain for both of them.

She was less certain what she was to do about her rapidly approaching marriage. The problem occupied her gloomy thoughts for most of the day, when she wasn't trying to wrest them away from far more dangerous ground.

It was sheer bravado that had made her assure Deveril her plans had not changed, for she was by no means certain that was true. Charles was a dear, but she was beginning to think that Deveril was right: perhaps he deserved better. Worse, she now knew she had been inexcusably naive to think she could give herself quite happily to a man she didn't love.

But she had known far less about passion then, she thought bitterly. And her brief taste of it since had taught her it was more a curse than a blessing.

She also knew that Charles's few kisses had been pleasant but had by no means left her feeling that she had been wholly consumed, as Deveril's did. She tried desperately to tell herself that that would change. She would grow to love Charles in time, for he was good and kind, and then she would forget that brief madness of the blood that was only half pleasant and half terrifying.

And call Deveril her brother-in-law, her own mocking voice reminded her. That was but another thing she had not counted on when she had agreed to become Charles's wife.

But despite Lucinda's obvious hopes, that was by no means certain. At any rate, to break off the engagement after it had been publicly announced would be humiliating for all parties concerned. And what grounds would she use? That she had allowed herself to be momentarily swept off her feet by a man who felt nothing toward her but contempt and had no honorable intentions at all where she was concerned? She feared even Deveril would find that laughable.

Worse, she had willingly undertaken this journey at Charles's expense, at the end of which everyone expected them to be married. Even were her reputation to survive the failure to do so, which was highly unlikely, she was not sure Charles's would. It would certainly tend to make them both a laughingstock.

And if she were mad enough to break the engagement, she would be back on the same old treadmill, only with some added difficulties thrown in. To remain in Brussels was clearly unthinkable, but between them she and Robin had scarcely a feather to fly with. Even traveling by public accommodation and the Channel packet would be expensive, and she very much doubted they could afford their passage home again.

They might, she supposed, live in retirement while they threw themselves on their grandmother's mercy and waited for her to send them the money to reach England again. But even that course was by no means certain. Christina had written to Barbara Foxcroft before they left, informing her of her trip abroad and her coming marriage, and her grandmother was likely to be far too angry at the moment to be inclined to be generous.

Oh, damn Deveril! Couldn't he see that she had very little choice but to go through with the marriage now? He was the only one likely to be pleased enough by the break to offer her any concrete help, and she thought she would die before she would take it from him. Which left her exactly back where she had started.

At the second stop Robin, whether out of mischief or not, declared himself bored and asked to change places with

Charles in Deveril's phaeton. Deveril looked as if it were
the last thing he wanted, but he could hardly refuse. And
so Robin climbed into the elegant vehicle when they once
more set out.

Christina mistrusted the arrangement, but like Deveril she
could find no reason to object. Robin had earlier expressed
admiration for Deveril's driving skill and had longed to get
a few pointers from him. She hoped that was in his mind,
but she could not rid herself of the suspicion Robin knew
more than he was letting on.

Christina wondered a little hysterically how they would
manage to pass the time together. From the beginning Robin
had seemed torn between his admiration for so notable a
figure and his loyalty to his sister, and Deveril had been polite
enough, but things were hardly likely to have improved in
the last twenty-four hours.

Then she refused to let herself worry about it. She had
had very little sleep the night before, and the tedium of the
trip was beginning to tell on her. Belgian roads were vastly
inferior to English ones, and even Deveril's luxurious coach
rocked and groaned over the uneven surface. Lady Danbury
complained they might as well be back at sea.

She promptly went back to sleep in her corner, and even
Lucinda was dozing, so Christina gratefully closed her own
eyes. She did not immediately sleep, however, for the
uncertainty of her future and the unpleasantness of the choice
that soon awaited her loomed larger with every mile they
covered.

She supposed if she asked Charles, he would lend her the
fare home, or perhaps even Lady Danbury, though both
would be justified in thinking they had been made to look
fools. As far as her chaperone was concerned Christina
suspected if she asked her advice, which she had no intention
of doing, she would receive extremely practical counsel on

the advisability of forgetting foolish scruples and marrying Charles with as little delay as possible.

Unfortunately, whereas before marriage had seemed merely a sensible solution, one born of reason and common sense, now it smacked too much of selling herself. And she knew she had Deveril to thank for that as well.

Sometime in the midst of weaving rather wild plans to remain in France and hire herself out as a governess, Christina fell asleep. But her dreams were even more fantastic than her waking thoughts, for she dreamed she was running away, both Charles and Deveril in hot pursuit of her. Which she was running from she didn't know, or perhaps it was both. But Charles begged her to stop, and Deveril merely grinned at her in that mocking, knowing way, his silver eyes gleaming unpleasantly as if he knew she would never escape him.

Then, incredibly, Charles pulled a pistol and began firing, though whether at her or Deveril she again couldn't tell. But his usually pleasant face was contorted with rage and he was screaming that they had betrayed him, both of them.

Christina woke, her heart pounding, to discover that part of her dream had been very real. Incredibly, the sound of a pistol still echoed in her ears and they had pulled to a stop, Lady Danbury and Lucinda beginning to look white and scared.

Deveril's curricle, in the meantime, had outdistanced the slower caravan by some miles. He still seemed on edge and had addressed only a few curt comments to his passenger.

Robin grinned, in no way put out. By no means blind, he had a good hunch what was going on. He was only uncertain what he should do about it. He did have affection for his sister, but he was basically indolent and unused to bestirring himself for others. And Christina was unlikely to thank him for interfering, if it came to that.

Robin might be far from approving of his sister's marriage to the worthy Charles, but still less did he wish to see her become Deveril's mistress. And that, unless he was much mistaken, was a very real danger. Robin toyed with the idea of informing Deveril that he would have him to reckon with if he tried to give his sister a slip on the shoulder. Then he grinned wryly at the mental image of such a scene. Deveril would undoubtedly damn his eyes for him, with justification, and Christina would be equally furious and probably not much less forthcoming on the subject.

But even less than Christina did Robin delude himself that Deveril would ever offer his sister marriage. Deveril's family was an old and extremely proud one, and Barbara Foxcroft seemed an insurmountable obstacle to any legitimate ending to the affair. Robin was out in the world far more than Christina, and he had few illusions. A man would have to be as besotted as Charles to risk allying himself in marriage with the granddaughter of such a one, for at the most it spelled social ruin, and at the least the unpleasant sniggering of all one's friends.

Well, Robin might believe Deveril wanted his sister, but he was unlikely to ever be described as besotted. And his determination from the begining to break up her betrothal to Charles betrayed his feelings on the subject.

That fact grimly acknowledged, Robin found himself unexpectedly in favor of his sister's marriage, and quickly, to the solid but dense Charles. She would doubtless never be deliriously happy, and, knowing her, bored within a few months of her marriage. But she would have achieved the respectability she sought, and, also knowing her, would never let Charles guess that her heart belonged elsewhere.

That being so, Robin was as eager for the journey to be over as his sister was reluctant. He had long since begun to regret his presence on so sedate a journey. He found Charles boring, Lady Danbury far worse, and not even the mild pleasure of flirting with Lucinda had withstood his realization that she had eyes only for Deveril.

In fact, at any other time the tangled relationships among the travelers would have been highly amusing. It was equally apparent to him that Deveril saw Lucinda as no more than a pleasant child. He had eyes only for Robin's, not Charles's sister, much as he tried to hide the fact. And Christina seemed to fully return the compliment; while in the meantime the saintly Charles continued to insist upon putting her up on a pedestal, where she didn't belong and had no desire to be, while blithely unaware of the intrigue going on right under his nose.

Oh, aye, highly amusing, no doubt. Except that Christina was likely to be confoundedly hurt before it was over.

At any rate, Robin had another reason for wishing the journey over—or at least that he had not been quite so drunk the night before they left. He had been in a reckless mood, engendered by being run off his legs and with no immediate hope of recruiting the ready any time soon; and even he could see that to put the touch to his new brother-in-law the moment the vows were exchanged would scarcely endear Charles to the married state, or help convince him that Christina had married him for anything but his money.

Whatever his reasons, he had been unexpectedly foolish, and he thought he would be glad to reach Brussels. It was his motto to get over heavy ground as easily as possible, and he feared they were soon to encounter a good deal of heavy ground.

In fact, he found that he was uneasy out of view of the coaches. He told himself he was being foolish, but nevertheless said with elaborate casualness to Deveril, "Perhaps we should turn back. The others will be wondering where we've gotten to."

Deveril glanced at him but made no reply. But at the first point the road widened, he obligingly turned his phaeton around.

For a moment Robin was filled with admiration at the skillful maneuver, for the road had not really been wide enough for such a turn. But for some reason anxiety drove him, and he merely contented himself with an appreciative grin and briefly wondered whether he dared ask Deveril for any pointers.

They had lost sight of Charles, too, who had left the execrable road to canter across the fields that lined it, saying he and the horse both needed the exercise. But they shortly caught him up as they retraced their way.

Charles pulled up and grinned. "Not bad country along here. Neat and civilized."

Robin agreed but again suggested they should return to the others. This time Deveril glanced at him rather more searchingly. Then he merely shrugged and drove on, Charles falling into an easy pace beside them.

They had gone something more than a mile when they heard a pistol shot in the silence. Robin swore and sat up, his attempt at unconcern leaving him, and Deveril too jerked his head up. He said something under his breath and then dropped his hands. His team shot forward, bouncing the phaeton dangerously on the abdominable road.

Charles had also started, then raced after them. The road was a winding one, and in frustration he shouted something to them and then abruptly left the road, taking again to the fields cross-country.

Then came a second shot, frighteningly near this time, and then a woman's blood-curdling screams.

Chapter 15

AT THE FIRST SHOT Christina had woken, her heard pounding, to find Lucinda looking very white and scared, and Lady Danbury, on whom the journey's frequent mishaps had not had a reassuring effect, alarmingly rigid.

The heavy coach had pulled to a lumbering halt amid shouted commands in French and slower English curses. His lordship's servants, it seemed, had been taken wholly by surprise.

After that first startled moment of fear, Christina was oddly calm. She did not doubt it was yet another of Deveril's tricks to force her to break her engagement to Charles, and if so it was the most inexcusable of all.

"My dear ma'am," she said urgently, trying to calm Lady Danbury's incipient hysterics, "pray don't distress yourself this way. It is nothing but a trick. I promise you we are in no danger."

But it was Lucinda who repeated in astonishment, "A *trick*? Whatever do you mean, Miss Castleford?" She was very pale and, Christina feared, not far from hysteria herself.

Instantly Christina realized her folly. But it seemed unconscionable to allow Lady Danbury to be made once more the victim of Deveril's cruel single-mindedness, and so she repeated in a low voice from which it was scarcely possible to hide her rage, "Yes. I can't explain now, but there is no reason to be afraid. They won't hurt us."

But Lucinda demanded shrilly, "Pray, how would you know what they intend? Are you in French highwaymen's confidence?"

Christina was by now sorry she had started it, but answered rather wearily, "I told you it is too complicated to explain now, but I am sure these men were hired by Deveril. They mean us no harm, they only mean to frighten us. There is no reason for alarm."

"Hired by Deveril!" gasped Lucinda, fear beginning to give way to outrage. "Are you out of your mind?"

Christina was almost glad there was time for no more. The next moment the door beside her had been wrenched open and a voice said roughly, in heavily accented English, "You will disembark quietly. If you do as you are told, nothing will happen to you."

She was tempted to refuse to climb down, but one look at her companions' faces showed that her attempt at reassurance had been as wasted as it was foolish. Lady Danbury almost fell down the steps, pleading all the time for them to spare their lives. Lucinda followed more slowly, looking unmistakably frightened.

There seemed little choice, so Christina followed them down onto the road, looking around her quickly. There were three men in sight, all heavily muffled: one at the horses' heads, another covering the driver and the postilions with a steadily held pistol, and the third waving another pistol at the three of them. There was no sign of the baggage vehicles or their three male escorts yet again. But then Christina thought sardonically that by now she hardly expected them to be there.

Having assured himself there were no other occupants of

the coach, the one nearest them seemed to find three women a negligible threat, for he lowered his pistol and spoke rapidly to one of his comrades. Then he said to them, in the heavily accented English they had first heard, "All your valuables, if you please. Do not try to hide anything or it will go very much the worse for you. Is this all your baggage?"

"Yes," said Christina coldly.

Lucinda started to correct her, then evidently thought better of it, for she weakly dropped her eyes.

"And where is your escort?" inquired their interrogator. "The English are all mad, *ça ce voir*, but even English demoiselles do not travel without a gentleman to escort them. Where is he?"

"We did not feel we needed one," said Christina, scarcely troubling to hide the contempt in her voice. "We were not aware we had anything to fear on the highways in broad daylight."

He laughed rather unpleasantly at that. "Then you were misinformed, *mademoiselle*. Your jewels and all your money, and quickly."

Lucinda, with a defiant look at Christina, said loudly, "We are indeed escorted, and they will be coming back at any minute. You would do better to leave us alone while you still have the chance."

Again he laughed, unperturbed by the threat. "In that case, I think I will give myself that honor. In the meantime, we will have a look through your baggage, *non*?"

He gestured to the one at the horses' heads, who came to join him, and together they began haphazardly pulling off the trunks that were strapped on behind. Without hesitation, ignoring the outraged cries of Lady Danbury, they broke open the locks and began tossing the contents of each out onto the road.

They seemed to find nothing to interest them (for, as

Christina privately thought in contempt, they had done enough damage for show) for the first one came back, waving his pistol, while the other one climbed into the coach and seemed to be searching it.

The one with the pistol said mockingly, "And now, *mademoiselles*, your valuables, if you please. And I think we will start with that very interesting necklace you are wearing, *madame*"—he waved his pistol toward Lady Danbury.

That lady turned even paler, if possible, for against the dictates of both taste and common sense she was wearing a very expensive necklace of diamonds and rubies. She had explained that it was the last gift her dear late husband had given her and she never went anywhere without it.

When she made no move to remove it, the man reached out a negligent hand toward it. It was the last straw. Christina had stood by in silent fury until now, but she was not prepared to watch Lady Danbury's jewels stolen for the sake of a feud that had nothing to do with her. She might have begun to regret that lady's presence on the journey, but she would not let her suffer on her account.

Fearlessly she knocked his hand away, crying furiously, "This farce has gone on long enough! I know who you are and who hired you. The game is over now."

Lady Danbury gave a little scream and fainted dead away. Lucinda cried out in horror, and the next moment Christina had been yanked against the man and held tightly, her arms pinioned to her sides. "You are brave, *mademoiselle*, but extremely foolish," he said in her ear. "But since you have chosen to interfere, I think you will be our hostage, to assure us of the return of our property. And, of course, anything else of value we may find."

His words made no sense, but she scarcely heard them anyway, for complete pandemonium broke out then. The coachman on the box gave a low growl and started to climb down, halted only by a warning from the pistol still trained on him. Then a solitary horseman had emerged from the fields to the front and left of them, giving a loud shout.

What he saw was enough to alarm anyone, with Lady Danbury lying unconscious in the road, their baggage opened and strewn about, and Christina struggling in the arms of a masked bandit.

At any rate the rider reacted instinctively and with admirable bravery. He did not hesitate but charged toward them unarmed.

What happened next seemed almost to occur in slow motion, and it was to haunt Christina for months to come. With alarm she recognized Charles even as she heard the rapid swearing in French of the man who held her. His arm tightened warningly on her, but his companion seemed more easily flustered. She watched in disbelief as the man holding the pistol on the coachman gave an exclamation and turned quickly. At sight of the figure on horseback charging down upon them at full speed, he raised his pistol and, evidently rattled, fired.

The report sounded abnormally loud in the warm afternoon, followed by Lucinda's scream of terror. Then, almost in slow motion, Charles faltered in the saddle, then pitched backward off his horse into the dust of the road and lay still where he had fallen.

The man holding her swore again and then, as the sounds of another vehicle approaching rapidly came to them, let Christina go and barked a sharp order. The three men mounted rapidly and rode off without a backward glance while Christina stood in stunned horror at what she had caused.

Lucinda gave a little moan and like Lady Danbury fainted dead away. Deveril's coachman swore with surprising fluency and rapidly dismounted from his high perch. But Christina was aware of none of them. She had remained frozen only a moment, then picked up her skirts and raced to where Charles lay on his back in the road.

What she discovered was enough to confirm her worst imaginings. There was a great deal of blood on the front of his coat and shirt, and her hand came away red. His eyes were closed and his face deathly pale.

But there was no time for squeamishness. She felt for the wound, only marginally aware of the noise behind her, as Lady Danbury recovered consciousness and commenced to engage in extremely noisy hysterics, and Deveril's servants exchanged shocked comments. Christina had managed to lodge her handkerchief tightly against the gaping hole she found in Charles's side when a harsh voice said above her, "Move over and let me see. This is no place for you."

She had not been aware of the arrival of Deveril's phaeton, but now at the sound of his voice she was filled with a rage that seemed to consume her. "You killed him! You killed him, damn you!" she cried shrilly, unaware of her tears which streamed down her face. "Are you finally satisfied?"

He didn't even bother to answer but thrust her roughly aside and began to staunch the flow of blood. When she in her irrational rage would have fought him, not wanting him to touch Charles, he said dampingly, "Get a hold of yourself! You're not a fool like Lady Danbury or Lucinda, and there's no time for that now. Find me something to pack the wound with and hurry!"

She knelt in the road for a moment longer, still only half rational, but his words had operated on her like an unwelcome cold shower. She still wanted to scream, scratch, and claw at him in a futile attempt to assuage her own guilt, but he was right. There was no time for that now.

She pushed herself to her feet, feeling as if she had been

ill for a fortnight, and made her unsteady way to the strewn baggage, hastily picking up whatever she found that would serve as bandages with no regard to value or ownership.

On the edge of her consciousness she registered that Robin was standing there, looking white, but it meant no more to her than that. The rest of them she didn't notice at all.

When she returned to Deveril, he had stripped off Charles's coat and was pressing the wound with Christina's handkerchief and his own cravat, which he had hurriedly pulled off. He scarcely glanced at her but took the objects she handed him. "Put your hand here and press as hard as you can," he barked at her.

Mindlessly she did as she was told, while Deveril quickly and efficiently tore the stuff she had handed him into strips for bandages. He then bound the strips tightly around Charles's chest with surprising skill.

Only then did he glance up at her, with her white face and bloodstained dress. "If you are done with your hysterics, get someone to help me carry him to the coach. We've got to find a doctor quickly."

She backed before him, again weakly doing his bidding, but fortunately Blackaby was already there, looking exceedingly concerned. Between them they lifted Charles's lifeless body and carried it to the coach.

Lady Danbury, at sight of their gory burden, began to wail even louder. It seemed that she feared the bandits would return any moment, and was demanding to be instantly conveyed to the next town, where she had every intention of returning to London and never setting foot out of it again.

Lucinda had recovered and was cowering in the road, white and shaken. Robin had gone to her, and at the sight of her brother she, too, buried her face in Robin's sleeve and gave way to a paroxysm of weeping.

They loaded Charles onto one of the seats, and then Deveril

turned and said shortly to Robin, ''I'm sorry to do this to you, but the other vehicles should be along shortly. You can then drive my rig. Blackaby tells me there is a village not too far ahead. You will find us there, unless it is necessary to go on to find a doctor, in which case I will leave word for you. Now we must go. There is not a moment to be lost.''

It took even Christina a moment to realize that he meant to drive off and leave them all standing there in the middle of the road. Lady Danbury was even slower on the uptake, but when it registered her jaw dropped, and she was for once shocked into welcome silence.

The next moment Christina had thrust herself up the stairs and said fiercely, ''I'm coming with you.''

He looked her over coolly. ''Very well. But only if you can be of some use. I have neither the time nor the patience to deal with hysterical women.''

Her mouth tightened in anger, and she climbed on into the vehicle. The next moment they had started, throwing her back against the squabs and provoking a piercing wail from Lady Danbury that he was leaving them there to be murdered by French cutthroats.

Christina occupied herself during the short, horrible drive by kneeling on the floor of the coach as best she could and wiping Charles's face clean of the dust of the road. His complexion was still dreadfully white and his eyelids did not flicker, but his skin was warm to the touch and she told herself he was not going to die. *He could not.*

She and Deveril exchanged not one word. For his part, Deveril maintained a steady pressure on his makeshift bandage and frequently checked Charles's pulse as if to reassure himself he were still alive.

It could not have been more than ten minutes—though it seemed like hours—before they reached the small French village, like so many others they had driven through, and pulled into the yard of a quaint-looking inn. The arrival of so grand a coach occasioned considerable notice from the local children, whose wonder was augmented by the coachman shouting to the lounging ostlers that there was a wounded man on board and they need a doctor quickly.

After that things happened in accelerated, not slow, motion. The landlady bustled from the house, full of exclamations and questions, and seemed a sensible woman. While a good many of the villagers stood around gaping, she took charge, ordering the preparation of her best bedchamber and dispatching her son for the doctor, who, as luck would have it, resided in the village not two houses away. She then bustled after as they carried the wounded man upstairs, issuing orders for a fire to be lit, water to be instantly boiled, and brandy to be fetched.

In an amazingly short time the doctor came running, looking spare and competent, with an immense black bag. He bent briefly over the victim, made a swift examination, then ordered the room emptied except for the landlady, whom it appeared had helped him in his surgery before.

The excitement over, those who had gathered below in the inn yard began to disperse, the servants who had had the slightest excuse to make a trip upstairs returned to their duties, and Christina found herself outside the door of Charles's room, forgotten and wholly unnecessary.

Fear was like a copper taste in her mouth, and suddenly it was all too much for her. She had never fainted in her life before and despised women who did, but the bright hall began spinning before her eyes and she was aware of a strange roaring in her ears.

The next moment Deveril had shoved her head down and said curtly, "Close your eyes and breathe deeply. There's no point in fainting now."

It was all she needed. Her head came up, the faintness

instantly forgotten, replaced by the rage she had felt earlier. "You!" she managed, stuttering a little in her bitter rage. "Did you mean to kill Charles, or was that just an accident? A regrettable little miscalculation in your plans?"

He frowned down at her, then looked quickly around and abruptly dragged her into an empty bedchamber. "What the devil are you talking about?" he demanded.

She laughed at that, and the sound was near to being hysterical even in her own ears. "The devil is what I'm talking about," she said wildly. "You vowed to best me anyway you could, with no thought to anyone else who might get in the way. Well, someone did, and now, if he dies, you will be little short of a murderer. Have you thought of that?"

He still retained his hand on her arm, and at that he almost shook her. "Don't be ridiculous," he snapped. "I didn't plan this."

"Do you expect me to believe that? You planned the accident to your coach, ignoring the presence in it of an wholly innocent bystander. You had my luggage deliberately lost overboard. You planned the mixup in rooms and even tried to seduce me when all else had failed. Do you really expect me to believe this wasn't just another attempt to frighten me into jilting Charles? The only thing I don't understand is what kind of man could do that with no thought to anyone else. For a while I had even foolishly begun to wonder—but you are the devil they call you. And whether or not Charles dies, I will never be able to forgive you. Never!"

He stood there a moment longer, a muscle jerking in his cheek. Then he turned and walked out without another word.

Chapter 16

THE REST of the party arrived a half hour later, in varying stages of shock and outrage. Robin found Christina waiting anxiously and said without preamble, "Good God, what a devilish coil."

Christina thought wearily that her brother's words were truer than he knew, but lacked the energy to rouse herself to anger anymore. After a moment Robin added, "I can get nothing but hysterics from either of my two charges. Do you, er, have any idea what the bandits were after?"

He looked a little strained, but Christina scarcely noticed. She only knew that was a subject she would not readily broach again, and so said wearily, "No. How are Lucinda and Lady Danbury?"

Robin made a face, rapidly recovering. "About as you might expect. Lady Danbury vows she will not sleep another night on French soil and demands to be taken home immediately. Deveril and I have both tried to point out to her that whatever happens she will have to spend at least one more night on French soil, for she can't be wafted magically home again, more's the pity, especially if she is to dally as long for dead calm seas as she did coming over. But she refuses even to set foot in the inn."

"Poor ma'am," said Christina blankly. "She didn't bargain for any of this, I fear. And Lucinda?"

"She's naturally all to pieces. In fact, Deveril thinks it best if she returns to England too. She can do nothing and is likely merely to make a nuisance of herself. So far she's done little but sit and cry. Lord, I didn't know females had so much water in 'em."

Christina raised her head at that, mildly astonished. "And did she consent to leave her brother?"

"Not in so many words. I told you all she will do is cry. Deveril's damned patient with her, I have to give him that. But he has already half made her see she will only be in the way, and that without a chaperone it would be extremely improper for her to remain. Give him another few minutes and he'll have her talked around. *I* am deputized to take you all back to London, by the way," Robin added sardonically.

"And who is to nurse Charles?" asked Christina sarcastically.

"Oh, the doctor assures Deveril there is an excellent nurse in the village, and the landlady seems to be a competent enough woman. And there will be Deveril himself, of course, who promises to stay here until Charles is well enough to return home."

"It seems Lord Deveril has been extremely busy," said Christina, rapidly shaking off her former stupor. "But you may tell him I, at least, am not leaving."

Robin looked annoyed but not particularly surprised. "Aye, I told him you were likely to prove difficult. But he's right, you know," he added bluntly. "You have no experience of the sickroom either, and as Deveril pointed out, conditions here are hardly ideal. It is no place for a gently bred woman, whether you or Lucinda."

"Nevertheless I am staying."

"Oh, don't be ridiculous," snapped Robin, surprisingly

suddenly at the end of his patience. "I should hardly need remind you that if it is improper for Lucinda to stay without a chaperone, it is doubly so for you. You have told me often enough that because of Grandmother you must never invite a hint of scandal to attach itself to you. What do you think you will be doing if you remain alone here with Deveril?"

"And did Deveril point that out as well?" she inquired ironically.

"No, he jolly well didn't. But he might as well have, for you may be sure it has already occurred to him."

"Then he may return with the rest of you if he fears his reputation may be tarnished. I am remaining with my fiancé, which must surely absolve me."

And from that stance he could not budge her. He at last went away muttering, and it was not long before Deveril himself knocked briefly on the door, then strode in. "What nonsense is this I hear?" he demanded without preamble.

She had half expected his coming, but it was a shock nonetheless to confront him. "I thought I made myself very clear to my brother. There does not seem to be any room for error."

He swore, then said flatly, "I am desolate to be obliged to contradict you, but you are going with the rest of them. It would be impossible enough were Lady Danbury staying, but since she is not, your presence here will cause nothing but trouble."

"That may have worked with Lucinda, my lord, but it fails signally with me," she said, fast descending from her Olympian calm. "I am staying, and there is nothing you can do to prevent me."

"You are mistaken. I can pick you up and place you bodily in that coach, and believe me, I won't hesitate if you leave me no other choice. Save your martyred act for later. You would be a hell of a nuisance and I will have my hands full enough without that, God knows.''

She had risen unconsciously and was now confronting him, her face white and her eyes blazing. ''*You* will have—? Under the circumstances your effrontery is nothing short of amazing.''

His face darkened again for a moment, then abruptly he ran a distracted hand through his hair and said more quietly, ''Look, Red, I know you are worried and upset—''

''Don't call me that!'' she fairly shrieked.

His face closed again. ''But Charles would be the first to wish you to return. I think you know that if you are honest with yourself,'' he finished grimly.

She gave a rather wild laugh. ''Honest? You dare to talk to me of honesty? I can only say that if you are worried for your own reputation, my lord, you needn't stay. We don't need you.''

''Then if reason will not work with you, you little fool, you leave me no other choice!'' he said, almost as angry as she. ''You are returning with your brother, and that's final.''

But she had the last word after all. ''And leave Charles to your tender mercies?'' she demanded with deadly intent. ''If nothing else, my lord, you will need a witness, for if he dies, I promise you I will not be silent until you are publicly named for the murderer you are.''

Once again he swore, and then turned without another word and left her.

It was Robin who returned some ten minutes later. ''I don't know what you said to Deveril,'' he said shortly, ''but he's looking like thunder and will say only that you have decided to remain.''

''Good,'' she answered indifferently, aware of little more at the moment than how long the doctor was taking.

Robin studied her for a moment, then shrugged. "Well, if you're bent on doing this, I can't stop you. Lady Danbury kicked up the predictable fuss, and Lucinda suddenly remembered her own duty and wavered for a few minutes, but Deveril has managed to convince them to go on. Are you sure you'll be all right?"

She had to make her distracted brain make sense of his words. "All right? Yes, of course I will be."

He sighed, as if aware of her preoccupation. "Well, then, I don't like to leave you, but I really think you will be better without Lady Danbury et al. I will be back as soon as possible. With any luck I'll meet Deveril's agent at Ostend and will be able to turn my charges over to him. But if not I may have to escort them all the way to London. Is there anything you need from there? Aside from clothes, that is."

She had completely forgotten her lack of wardrobe, and made herself try to deal with such mundane matters, though she did it very badly. All the time her ears strained for a sound from the room across the hall, and she was beginning to shake so badly it almost felt as if she had the ague. She commissioned Robin to bring what clothes of hers still remained at Lady Danbury's, and what money he could manage, for she refused to be beholden to Deveril in any way. "And . . . and lemons, please," she added rather distractedly. "As many as you can manage. When—if"—her voice almost broke, but then she forced herself to go on—"Charles recovers, he will like to have lemonade to drink, and I fear they will not be available locally."

Robin frowned, not overly pleased by the commission, but for once forebore to protest. "He'll be all right," he insisted optimistically. "Lord, Kit, try to pull yourself together. If you are going to stay and nurse him, it won't do any good for you to work yourself into a decline."

"No. No," she said, and tried to smile, though it was a

pitiful effort. "Don't worry about me. I shall be fine."

"Oh, I know that. Um, look. I hate to bring it up, but do you still have that package I gave you to hold for me?" he asked with elaborate casualness.

Usually she was attuned to all his games and would have been instantly suspicious, but she was too distraught now to pay him close attention. She thought she had at last heard voices out in the hall and was on pins and needles to be away. "What? Package? No, of course not. I thought you knew. It must be at the bottom of the Channel by now."

Robin stared at her for a long moment, then threw back his head and began to laugh.

It had indeed been the doctor that Christina had heard, and he reported to her that he had been able to extract the ball from *Monsieur's* wound without much difficulty. The patient was now resting as comfortably as could be expected.

As for the prognosis, he naturally could not be held to it at this early time, but he saw no need at the moment for undue pessimism. Undoubtedly the lung had been affected, and the patient was gravely ill. But he was a *jeune homme* in the best of health, it would appear, and so should with any luck make a full recovery. He understood she was the fiancée of the patient and meant to remain to nurse him? Ah, good. Good. He would need most careful nursing, no doubt, though she could with confidence rely upon the woman he would send from the village. She need only give him the tisane he would leave whenever the patient regained consciousness—which would probably not be for several hours—and keep him quiet. He himself would be back in the morning, and she might place the utmost reliance upon his desire to serve so ravishing an English demoiselle.

Christina thanked him blindly, again feeling so faint that it was all she could do to return his many compliments. When he had at last bowed himself off, she leaned her face gratefully against the cool wall, aware of the room swimming around her, and tried to keep her stomach from belatedly rebelling.

Once more it was Deveril who rescued her. One moment she was aware of nothing but her whirling head and the bitter taste of nausea, the next he had ordered curtly behind her, "Here, drink this."

When she didn't instantly respond, he said something violent under his breath and turned her, his hand hard on her arm, and himself carried the glass to her lips.

She was too dizzy and confused at the moment to protest, and so weakly swallowed some of the liquid. Instantly she gasped, realizing it was not claret he had brought her this time but far more potent brandy. It burned in her throat, snatching her breath away, and then left a raw path down to her stomach.

But as she tried to protest he ruthlessly tipped some more down her throat, and she was obliged to admit that it helped. In a moment her head had cleared and a little warmth seemed to return to her limbs, which she had begun to fear were permanently frozen.

When he saw that she was looking a little better he pressed the glass into her hand. "Finish this and then go and lie down for a while," he said in his autocratic way. "Charles will sleep for hours and doesn't need you, and if you intend to be useful, it will do no good to prostrate yourself on the first day."

He had gone before she could either thank him, which she had no intention of doing, or protest at his high-handedness. After staring after him helplessly, she retired to her room and burst violently into overwrought tears.

Robin found her there shortly before they left. In his boots and greatcoat he looked, suddenly, much more mature than she remembered him. But he halted in the doorway in almost comical dismay at her unaccustomed tears. "Kit, good God! This is not like you."

"I k-know," she managed, unable to stop or pull herself together. "D-don't mind me. It is just sh-shock, or something."

He went to put his arm clumsily around her, looking troubled. "I—yes, of course. But, well, I—do you really love him that much? I have to admit I thought you were marrying him merely to escape from Grandmother."

She managed to raise her head then and make an effort to dry her tears. "Love him?" she repeated hollowly. "I fear I am being anything but noble. If Charles dies it will be my fault."

Chapter 17

ROBIN and the party he was escorting left soon afterward, and from her window Christina heard the noisy sound of their departure. She tried not to feel as if her last support had abandoned her, and since she was indeed exhausted, after that she slept fitfully for about an hour, trusting that Charles would not waken. Then she rose, feeling like a ghost, and went to check on him.

It was to set the pattern for the next week, for the outside world seemed to shrink to two rooms. Her own bedchamber was a place she retired only when exhaustion forced her, and then she would lay dozing uneasily, half an ear cocked for the needs of her patient and troubled by tumbled, unpleasant dreams. The rest of the time she spent in the sickroom, tending to Charles or sitting by his side as he lay sleeping, only part of her mind on the book she was reading.

It also set the stage for one of the two bitter quarrels that sprang up between her and Deveril, and which showed no signs of being resolved. About midnight Deveril had walked into the sickroom himself, only to stop in astonishment at sight of her.

The woman from the village sent as nurse, Madame Ligny, seemed competent enough, but Christina had sent her away to eat and get what sleep she could. It would take all their combined strength to nurse Charles around the clock, and she had little doubt the woman had already put in a full day before she came. It was too much to expect her to sit up all night as well.

But Deveril was in no mood for explanations. He demanded to be told where the nurse was, and then looked anything but appeased at the answer. "Thank you, but I didn't hire her, nor did I allow you to stay so that you should sit up all night," he said forcefully, his anger in no way diminished by having to speak in a low voice. "If we need another nurse, then I shall hire one."

It was the first time they had met since his rescue of her, and it was all she could do to remain in the same room with him. "You may naturally do as you please," she said disdainfully, her words dripping ice. "Though I doubt you will be able to find another skilled nurse in so small a village. At any rate, it will be necessary to spell whoever you hire."

"I am aware of that," he snapped, evidently keeping his temper in rein only by the greatest of effort. "My valet has experience in a sickroom, and I am available when needed."

"You!"

She could not have expressed her opinion more clearly, and his face darkened unpleasantly. "Yes, of course me. However touching this display may be, my dear, you seem to forget that Charles is my oldest friend."

"Then it is a pity you didn't remember that sooner, my lord," she countered unforgivably. "At any rate, whatever you may choose to do makes no difference to me. I am not leaving."

He swore, briefly and succinctly, and walked out without another word. She was left to wonder why her victory seemed so hollow.

But mostly she had little time for thinking, which was just

as well. Despite the French doctor's comfortable prognosis, Charles was very ill indeed, and soon neither of them had much energy left for arguing. His lung was indeed affected, and the infection that set in had him running a dangerously high fever and delirious half of the time.

They managed, with painstaking politeness on both sides, to work out a schedule, for after that last confrontation Deveril had as little interest in her company as she had in his. Christina would sit with Charles during the day, spelled by Deveril and the kindly landlady when necessary, and the nurse in the village and Lacock, Deveril's extremely proper valet, split the night shift between them.

That was at Deveril's flat insistence, and Christina lacked the energy to fight him. At any rate, Charles seemed to grow more restless during the daytime, when the inn was busy and the noise evidently disturbed him. He was not yet fully conscious, but he seemed to find comfort in her presence and often clung feverishly to her hand, turning his head fitfully on the pillow seeking a cooler spot.

At any rate, it little mattered, for she was sleeping poorly and usually spent at least part of the night sitting in a chair by Charles's bedside, her thoughts a tangled web of guilt and horror.

If Charles died, she knew she would never be able to forgive herself. However much she might hate Deveril, in the more rational part of her mind she knew that it had been nothing more than an unfortunate accident, one that she bore almost as much blame in as he did. Despite her harsh accusations to Deveril and his undoubted culpability, it was impossible to deny that if she hadn't interfered, none of it would have happened.

Then there was her betrayal of Charles and those moments of madness with Deveril to add to her burden of guilt. What she would herself do in the future, whether or not Charles

recovered, was too distant even to bother about. If he died—
but that did not bear thinking about. And if he recovered,
whether she would still marry him or not—or whether he
would even still want her after he knew the truth, which she
was determined he should—seemed of little moment. She
dared think no further ahead than the time for the next dose
of medicine and the visit from the kindly French doctor.

Deveril, coming in once to relieve her, caught her in such
a moment when her guilt and fear almost combined to
overpower her. His mouth thinned and his face took on the
look of a thundercloud at the sight of the silent tears streaming
down her cheeks. But for once he wisely forebore to say
anything.

In fact, he was behaving in exemplary fashion, for him.
They seldom met except in passing, and then he treated her
with a distant courtesy that denied as effectively as she was
trying to those unforgivable moments between them. And
he proved to be an unexpectedly good nurse, both calm and
surprisingly patient. He tended to Charles's needs with a
minimum of fuss, was a soothing presence in the sickroom,
and could easily lift and turn him, whereas Christina had to
struggle to straighten his tangled sheets or sponge him to keep
the fever down.

Deveril caught her at that once as well and came instantly
to help her. And though the frown between his heavy brows
deepened and she could tell he was displeased, he again held
his tongue. He merely lifted Charles easily, allowing her to
tighten the sheets beneath him, and said harshly, "If you
need help, ask for it."

But Christina had learned her lesson as well, and so merely
bowed her head and made no reply.

Unfortunately, she was not so docile over the cause of the
second major blowup between them.

That had been occasioned by the loss of her wardrobe.

Without Lucinda to borrow from, she had shortly found herself in dire straits, particularly since her hours were so irregular and the village far too small for her to buy what she most urgently needed, even if she had had the money with which to do so.

But she would have died before acknowledging the problem to Deveril, and so did the best she could, washing out her dress and linen every night and borrowing a nightshift from the landlady.

They met so seldom, and were both so preoccupied when they did, she doubted Deveril even noticed, but on the third day of their stay she returned to her room at dusk, so emotionally and physically spent it was all she could do to drag one foot before the other, to find numerous boxes on the bed.

She stared at them in blank astonishment for a moment. Then, when she opened one to find dresses, shifts, and shawls, all the requirements of a young lady of fashion, her exhaustion fell away, to be replaced by rage. Without thinking she gathered up the boxes and stormed back to Charles's room, for she had no doubt who had provided them.

"Damn you," she cried, forgetting their tenuous truce and even the patient. "If you think I am going to wear anything of your providing, you are mistaken. I would rather die first!"

This time he remained coldly calm, which she was later to acknowledge placed her at a distinct disadvantage. He rose coolly at her entrance and drew her out of the room. Then he said deliberately in a low voice, "No doubt. But your ostensible reason for remaining is to help Charles. And since that purpose will not be served by the ridiculous constraints you have been reduced to in the last few days, no doubt hoping that I wouldn't notice, it would seem there is no more to be said.''

She was by no means so ready to abandon the battle. ''You are very right,'' she said, dumping the boxes at his feet. This time it was her turn to sweep out.

The next morning when she awoke, she found the boxes neatly stacked in her room again. She dressed with shaking hands and went straight to renew the battle.

This time she found Deveril in the coffee room, eating a solitary breakfast. Unfamiliar with his stated matutinal prejudices and the fact that he seldom willingly breakfasted before noon, she was unimpressed to find him there at eight o'clock in the morning and launched the attack immediately.

''If you find this charade amusing, my lord, I do not,'' she said contemptuously. ''I have told you exactly what you can do with the things you bought.''

He rose and bowed somewhat ironically, then deliberately poured her out a cup of coffee. ''Good morning, Miss Castleford. I trust you slept well?''

''I don't want any,'' she snapped. ''And if I find those boxes in my room again, I warn you I shall throw them out the window.''

He strolled over to the window to look out, seemingly unaffected by her temper, which only made her angrier. ''That would no doubt amuse the villagers, but frankly, Miss Castleford, I find these scruples as tedious as they are inexplicable,'' he drawled in a bored tone. ''Especially since you have been at some pains to point out, quite correctly, that the loss of your trunks is directly attributable to me.''

''You may think whatever you please!''

Again he bowed. ''Thank you. But if it will make you feel any better, you may call them a loan to Charles. He will undoubtedly reimburse me as soon as he is able.''

She longed to slap his face. "And do you think that makes it any better? But then, you needn't answer. I should know your opinion of me by now."

"I doubt that you do," he said dryly at last. "But what has that to do with anything?"

"Oh, nothing. All you need to know is that I have made up my mind and that is my last word on the subject."

She started somewhat blindly toward the door and was startled to find him suddenly there before her, barring her way. The sham of disinterest had completely fallen away, and his curious silver eyes were blazing down at her. "And this is mine, Miss Castleford," he pronounced in a deceptively calm voice. "You will wear the things in those boxes if I have to burn every stitch you stand up in and dress you myself. Is that understood? If you think I am bluffing, just try me."

What would have been the outcome of the ugly scene she was fortunately never to know, for the maid came in then to fetch the English lord more coffee. Christina, aware of her burning cheeks and the maid's avid curiosity, cursed the timing. She was fully aware that their unusual arrangements had aroused speculation among the far more earthy French, who evidently sensed an intrigue, and she was not prepared to add still more to their gossip. So she had no choice but to mutter an excuse and withdraw.

When she returned to her room, she found the landlady herself, Madame DuBois, hanging the last of the new things in her wardrobe. "Ah, *mademoiselle*," she exclaimed happily, "such beautiful new things, are they not? Milord has explained to me how your trunks were lost in an unfortunate accident, and I was delighted to oblige him in obtaining these replacements for you. Alas, it is not the same as if they had come from Paris, you understand, but now that the war is finally over, I think they are not too bad, eh?

Ah, but it would seem your journey has been fraught with mishaps, no? First the accident to your trunks, then this unfortunate affair. But the doctor tells me your fiancé is doing as well as can be expected, and that is at least good news, no?''

Christina knew she had lost. In the face of the landlady's simple curiosity, she could not now disdain Deveril's purchases without arousing even more speculation. At any rate, she had to admit that she was sorely feeling the loss of her trunks, for her one dress remaining was scarcely fit to be seen by now.

And so, hating him, the next morning she gave in and dressed herself in one of the gowns of his providing before she went in to check on Charles. And as worse luck would have it, she met Deveril in the hall on the way. He had to have noticed her capitulation, but if she had expected him to gloat, for once he disappointed her. He merely wished her a polite good morning and went on downstairs, leaving her to feel absurdly deflated.

But the battle was to resume shortly enough on another front. She still was sleeping badly and had become aware that she was hardly looking her best. There were dark shadows under her eyes, and her skin had taken on a translucent quality that even to her looked unhealthy. Madame tut-tutted over it and insisted upon making her a tisane before bedtime, but in fact Christina did not drink them and only the local nurse knew exactly how many nights she still spent at Charles's bedside, unable to sleep and finding an odd comfort there.

Then one night sometime after midnight, Deveril found her in the sickroom. She had not been aware he had gotten into the habit of checking on Charles as the last thing he did before going to bed.

Entering in his shirt sleeves, he stopped at sight of her,

and for a moment the silence stretched between them. Then he said flatly, "This extreme devotion no doubt does you credit, Miss Castleford. But it will do none of us any good, least of all Charles, if you make yourself seriously ill. Go back to bed at once, and I shall give orders you are not to be admitted again in the nighttime."

Instantly all her bitter grievances against him rose up to crowd out her reason, or the knowledge that it was foolish to cross him. "*You* will not—?" she gasped. "I have had about enough of your arrogance, my lord. This is not London and we are not all your lowly serfs to order about as you will. I sometimes think your reputation has indeed gone to your head, for you seem to believe you have only to order and everyone instantly snaps to do your bidding. Well, I am one who will never do your bidding, and you have no power over me at all. None! You may have forced me to wear your clothes and to put up with your presence over these past days, but it goes no further than that."

He had leaned back against the door frame and crossed his arms over his chest, looking dangerously relaxed. "Ah, I thought it would not be long until we were back to that again. You have been longing ever since to throw them back in my face, haven't you? But at least you possess some sense, which I admit I was beginning to doubt, for you haven't quite dared, have you?"

She knew it was folly to taunt him, but at the time she was unable to help herself. "Dared? You will find out what I dare, my lord. And how little I care for your orders and demands. I will see Charles when I choose, and there is not a thing you can do to stop me."

He pushed away from the doorway, still showing that dangerously deceptive casualness, though she could see that a little muscle had begun to beat in his lean cheek. "Can't I?"

She resisted the urge to back before him. "No. You don't frighten me, my lord, devil though you may be."

"Then you are a fool," he said through his teeth, "for I should frighten you, Miss Castleford." Before she could prevent him he had picked her up bodily and strode out the door.

Chapter 18

WILDLY FURIOUS, but unwilling to raise the house, Christina had no choice but to submit to his manhandling. But as soon as she was on her feet again in her own bedchamber, she spat at him, "Don't you ever, *ever* dare to touch me again. Do you hear me?"

"Oh, yes, I hear you," he retorted. "But I fear I'm unimpressed, despite the devotion you've been at such pains to display this past week."

"How—how dare you?"

"Oh, I dare a great deal, as you already know. I'm the devil, remember? But I'm curious about one thing. Is it me you're trying to convince by this touching display that you really love Charles, or yourself?"

She couldn't help it. She struck him before she could prevent herself, her hand flashing up and connecting with his jaw in a solid slap that left her hand stinging and a harsh red imprint on his face.

For a moment she was again appalled at what she had done, for no one had ever been able to drive her to physical violence before. She also was afraid he might return the favor in kind. But though his eyes were glacial, he merely bowed ironically and made to leave her.

Suddenly all the fight went out of her. The violence she was capable of—that only he seemed able to drive her to—had at last shocked her to her senses. It was true that she seemed scarcely to know herself any longer. The woman she had been, calm and rational, seemed no longer to exist. And she could no longer hide from herself the fact that her conduct since they had met was scarcely more excusable than his own inexcusable behavior.

Or perhaps she simply no longer had the strength left to fight him—or herself—any longer. "I'm sorry," she said weakly, closing her eyes and drooping exhaustedly. "I don't seem to know myself anymore. The things I've said and done in the past week are unforgivable."

He had halted at the door, though his expression did not change. Had she had the strength left to notice it, there was an oddly watchful look about him, as if for the first time he was uncertain of himself. "Not unforgivable," he said at last, surprising her. "Perfectly natural, under the circumstances. And if you don't know yourself, I think I am finally coming to."

She lifted her head at that, suspecting an unpleasant undermeaning. "Are you? I fear you may be right. Since I have known you, I seem to have been at pains to display every disagreeable trait you expect in me." Unconsciously she lifted her arms to flex her tired shoulders, unaware the candlelight behind her turned her hair to flame and silhouetted her body in its thin nightrobe.

Abruptly he turned away. She read in it condemnation and said even more wearily, "I can't blame you for despising me. I blamed you for everything, when I am at least as guilty as you. More perhaps, especially for Charles's accident."

He turned back again rapidly at that. "And what the devil is that supposed to mean? What nonsense are you spouting now?"

"Not nonsense. I blamed you for Charles's accident because I dared not blame myself. If—if he dies, I shall be responsible, not you."

He strode to her and put his hands on her soft shoulders, bruising her, ruthlessly shaking her until her head lolled. "Stop that!" he ordered. "I've never heard such twaddle in my life."

"Why? Because it's true?" She made no attempt to pull away from his hurting hands. "I have had to live with it for the past week. I don't lie to myself just because I don't like the answers."

His eyes rested on her in his hard way. "Don't you?" he demanded cruelly. "But that's exactly what you're doing now."

As she gasped, he added deliberately, "But you don't care to face that, do you? All this guilt and sudden devotion during the past week have been to disguise one thing and one thing only. Did you really think I wouldn't guess?"

She was struck dumb, daring neither to resist nor answer him. When she still remained passive under his hands he shook her again as if she were a rag doll. "Not that you were responsible for his being wounded, but that you have discovered for yourself that you don't love him. Haven't you? *Haven't you?*"

"No," she moaned. "No."

"Yes! I will readily admit that I have not been blameless in this affair. But you are every bit as black as I first believed you, for you are prepared to blindly wed a man you don't love and who will bore you within a few weeks for the sake of spiting me. We are two of a kind, my girl, and it's long past time you were made to acknowledge the fact."

"No. No!"

But he was still holding her by the arms, his face thrust close to her own, his eyes ruthless. "You weren't responsible for his being wounded any more than I was. But you are responsible for believing him capable of wanting you under such circumstances.''

"No!'' Too late she tried helplessly to pull away. "Whatever you say and whatever you would like to believe, Charles does love me, and I . . . love him. If I ever doubted that before, I have learned how true it is in this last week.''

"Then it is a weak and milk-fed passion,'' he said scathingly. "Believe me, Charles deserves far better. As for Charles loving you, of course he does. Exactly as he has loved half a dozen women before he met you and will half a dozen more after you have disappeared from his life.''

"And that is all that really matters, isn't it?'' she cried bitterly. "That you get your way?''

He looked as if he wanted to shake her again. "My way?'' he laughed a little wildly. "That's almost amusing. I have had to stand by for the last week and watch you piously tending and weeping over a man you don't love, out of some absurd guilt and whatever other misguided emotions of loyalty and defiance there may be in that stubborn, mixed-up red head of yours. And all the while I have had to make myself keep my hands off you, whether to strangle you or make love to you until you admit that you are mine and have been since the first moment I saw you—both of which I have badly wanted to do.''

This time she did manage to break his hold on her and backed away from him. "And that's what all of this has been about, hasn't it?'' she demanded in contempt. "You still haven't forgiven me for that first evening, or for preferring Charles to you. But I would have thought even you would have some honor. Or is this the way you treat your best friend while he is lying too ill to defend himself?''

"Don't talk to me of honor, my sweet,'' he said dangerously, once more advancing on her. "Not while you still bear the marks of my hands upon you. You do, don't you, however much you've tried to hide them."

Again she tried to back before him, but this time he was too quick for her. In a flash he had caught both her wrists and bared the fading bruises on the white flesh covered by the lace of her soft lawn nightrobe.

"Or did you mean to wed Charles with the marks of my lovemaking still on you?" he blazed.

She closed her eyes and swayed dizzily. She wanted to shout that that had been violence, not lovemaking, and that she never wanted to lose control of herself that way again. But she was too weary and too ashamed to fight him any longer.

Then, far more shocking than any further violence would have been, she felt the feather-light touch of his lips against her inner wrists, and then his tongue.

Fighting was one thing, survival another, and her eyes flew open in horrified self-preservation. She jerked her wrists away as if they had been burned, knowing that if she ever once gave in to him she would be lost. "No, no! I do love Charles!" she cried desperately. "I do, despite anything you may say. I love his gentleness, his easy good nature, his kindness. *He* had the tolerance to overlook my past when all you or most people could see was my grandmother's reputation. I will always love him for that."

But his temper left him as suddenly as it had come. "My sweet, hen-witted widgeon, those are precisely the things I love in Charles as well," he said wearily. "But they are hardly the basis for a marriage. Haven't you learned in all these weeks that for all his easy good nature, Charles's emotions are only skin deep?"

"That's not true. You're only saying that."

"It is true," he insisted with a lack of passion that was oddly convincing. "I have known him all his life. When we were children he was apt to adopt every hungry, mistreated mongrel that wandered by because of his soft heart. But he quickly lost interest once they became sleek and well fed again. I can't count the number I ended up with after he had tired of them.''

"No," she moaned. But even as she said it, the horrible truth of his words were seeping in. *Had* it only been a desire to rescue her, to prove to the world that he was not as prejudiced and cold-hearted as everyone else? Could that explain his sudden infatuation and willingness to overlook all her shortcomings?

As if aware of her thoughts, Deveril said more gently, with a pity that she despised coming from him, "My poor Red, don't look like that. He means it sincerely at the time, I promise you.''

She raised her head, pride coming belatedly to her rescue. "Why didn't you . . . tell me that earlier?" she inquired bitterly, "it might have succeeded where all your plots failed.''

He shrugged. "Would you have believed me? At any rate, I haven't told you now to hurt you, whatever you may think, but to prove a point. Surely even you, with the blinders you have deliberately worn—and which I'll admit I did much to encourage, in my iron-fisted way—must have begun to see during the trip that Charles doesn't really know anything about you. He sees your beauty and your unfortunate background, but not the stubbornness or that damnable pride of yours, not to mention the temper you manage to hide so well in his presence.''

"I never had a temper before I met you!" she interrupted bitterly.

He merely laughed as if pleased by the comment, which was by no means what she had intended. "As for the passion only half hidden under that cool exterior you show the world, you needn't tell me you never had that either before you knew me," he added unforgivably. "And both should tell you something. Charles wouldn't recognize it, and believe me, he wouldn't know what to do with it if he did. Haven't you yet learned that he's one of the men of this world who prefers not to have to deal with any undercurrents? Your passion and fire are merely likely to disconcert him. I can say this because I've known him all his life and appreciate him for what he is. But what he isn't is man enough to handle you, sweetheart, and it's long since time you faced the truth."

"The truth!" she countered bitterly, though she had the numbing feeling that he was right. "What do you know of the truth? This is yet another plot to get your way, because everything else you've tried has failed. But this one will too. I'm going to marry Charles whatever you say. And you can go to hell!"

"I think I've already been there this past week," he said surprisingly, his face tightening and his silver eyes growing bleak.

Then he lifted them and pinned her in their silvery glare. "And since you are such an unexpected coward, you force me to take you with me. I swore to let you both willfully ruin your lives without any further compunction, thinking if you are both such blind fools you deserve each other. Most of all I swore never to touch you again, especially while Charles was unable to defend himself. And that should amuse you."

But she looked very far from wanting to laugh.

He gave her no time to answer but went on inexorably, "But you force me to break even that vow, my sweet. It has been bad enough watching you immolate yourself on the altar of what you see as your guilt, but at least you will not be able to claim you did it not knowing the alternatives. Come here."

Again she backed before him, not quite able to keep the panic out of her eyes. "I know the alternatives, thank you. It was—you made me . . . that wasn't me, that clawing, scratching animal. It makes me ashamed to even think of it. I don't ever want to lose control like that again."

He laughed and reached lazily for her, once more very sure of himself. "You mean for once you felt and reacted, forgetting all your safe plans for the future. As you did the night we first met, when you fascinated me so. On at least those two occasions you forgot your determination to prove to the world you're nothing like your grandmother, didn't you?"

"I am nothing like my grandmother," she swore.

"My poor Red, you're far more like her than you know. She may have been immoral, but by God she knew what she wanted and took it with both hands. I find her distinctly admirable."

"And you've done everything in your power to prevent her granddaughter from marrying your best friend," she countered acidly.

He shrugged. "That—I will admit that was primarily out of pique. If I had not seen you and wanted you for myself, I would hardly have gone to such lengths, believe me. But enough of this talk. It is only delaying the inevitable. And I think we both know what that is."

She did. The house was silent and long asleep, and she knew this time there would be nothing to save her. No storm or dash of cold water to bring her to her senses. But still she tried to resist it, not even caring now that she betrayed herself with every word. "No. No, I beg you."

"What, begging, my sweet?" he mocked, sparing her no sympathy. "That's not like you." And then he reached out for her.

In unreasoning panic she tried to flee. Laughing, he caught

her easily and pulled her ruthlessly to him. "Will you fight me again this time? Or has all the fight gone out of you at last? Yes, I believe it has. However we both may fight it, we belong together. For better or worse, we're two sides to the same coin. I recognized that from the first night, I think. The Devil and his lady."

Chapter 19

CHRISTINA made no resistance as he lowered her to the waiting bed. She felt numb, hardly aware of his dark face above her or the possessive menace in his eyes.

She knew she would lose everything if she gave in to him now, for she had no illusions that this was anything more than another of his ruthless tricks. He might feel a transient lust for her, but he had never lost sight of his main goal. And he had made it more than obvious that he would stop at nothing to prevent her from marrying his best friend.

And what better way to make the marriage impossible? To prove that she was indeed no better than her grandmother, so that even Charles would be forced to acknowledge it? He was indeed a devil and she should have despised him.

But she was beyond that, for she was too busy despising herself. Whatever his motives, a few of Deveril's harsh words had taken unexpected seed, and she was at last facing the truth of her own motivations and actions.

He had said she was more like her grandmother than she cared to admit, and, God help her, the truth could no longer be denied. Not because she had been awakened to passion when she had least expected it, and behaved in a way she had despised at the time. But because she had cold-bloodedly set out to bargain her youth and beauty exactly as Barbara Foxcroft had done.

It little mattered that she had sought only respectability and peace. Or that she had meant to make Charles a good wife. She had looked down on and blamed her grandmother all of her life, when the only difference between them was the terms of the bargain. Her grandmother had held out for royalty and wealth, while she had demanded the far more modest price of a ring for her capitulation. But in the end she feared Barbara Foxcroft had been the more practical one, for security was far more easily bought than respectability. It seemed she had been both immoral and foolish, which should have been amusing after all her carefully laid plans.

And now Deveril meant to make it impossible for her to marry Charles, which should also have been amusing. Had he but known it he might have saved himself the trouble, for she knew now she could never marry Charles. Deveril had already won.

But he could not know that, of course, and was angry that she had somehow managed to slip away from him. His hands tightened on her face, and he growled, "No, you won't elude me that way either, my sweet. You will not hide inside your mind or pretend I'm someone else. When I take you, you will know it's me, and you will want me as much as I want you."

When she stubbornly made no answer, refusing either to give in or show any fear, his hands tightened until they caused physical pain. At last, unwillingly, her eyes flew to his, some of her passivity leaving her.

His smile seemed evil to her. "That's better. Now kiss me."

It wasn't working. The numbness was leaving her, along with her certainty of the answers she had reached. He was bent on nothing more than conquering her, she knew that.

But his hands and his silvery eyes boring into her were awakening too many memories. She wanted to blot out his eyes, along with the memories, but when she tried his hands tightened yet again, forcing them open.

Without meaning to she opened her mouth and moaned. "No, no . . ."

It must have been what he wanted to hear, for his hands relaxed slightly and there was triumph in his eyes. "Yes, damn you! I'll put Charles out of your head if I have to force him out bodily. When I am through with you, you will never again think of marrying him."

She wanted to laugh again, for it was all so unnecessary. But his nearness, his hands and eyes and his dark face so close to her own were doing strange things to her breathing. She wanted to strike out at him, and at the same time she wanted to bring that dark, triumphant face nearer, stroke the tumbled black hair back from his forehead. He looked freer, different than she had ever seen him. Except for that one momentous occasion she had only seen him dressed formally and elegantly, even tending to Charles. But now his hair fell forward over his face, and his shirt was open halfway down his chest. He looked unfamiliar and even more dangerous for some reason.

And, experienced as he was, he must have seen the longing in her eyes, for he laughed. "Yes, Red. Don't fight it any longer. I told you we were two sides to the same coin. Now say my name."

Still she resisted. "No, no—"

"Say it!"

"Deveril. Deveril, damn you!"

"That's better." He still held her head between his hands, as if even now he might give way to violence and crush her skull between them. But his eyes were on her lips and he added, "And now my first. Say it. You know what it is."

Everything that had ever been or was yet to be between them faded away, leaving only that moment and his body half on top of hers, his eyes holding hers so that she could not escape. "Say it," he murmured more softly, his eyes still on her lips and his hands beginning to caress her face. "Say it . . ."

The sweet cajolery won where the order could not, and she closed her eyes and whispered weakly, "Blaise . . . Blaise . . . oh, God."

And as if that had been the signal he needed, he groaned and swooped to take her mouth. But where before he had been cruel and hurtful, intent only on subduing her, now he seemed equally intent on forcing her to come the whole way of her own free choice. And she thought that was even crueler. His lips teased and taunted hers, and his hands soothed back the red hair from her face as if she were something infinitely precious to him.

And she knew she was indeed lost. She might have held out against his demands but not against his wholly unexpected gentleness. She moaned again and reached for him, everything forgotten but the need he was arousing in her.

There was a whisper of sound, as if he sighed, and then he was kissing her, and there was no room for any other thought. Only need and wonder, for she had thought he'd taught her something of passion before. But now she discovered that she had everything to learn. . . .

And, surprisingly, he could not have been a better tutor. Now that he had obtained her complete capitulation, he seemed content with that, for he was gentle and infinitely patient with her. When she thought she would faint with breathlessness from his kiss, he held her tightly and soothed her until she had regained her scattered senses. And when his hand first went to the neck of her nightrobe and she stiffened, momentarily afraid once more, he moved it and began to kiss her once more.

And in the end his patience paid off, for the next time his hand went to the ribbons at her throat she was beyond protest. And when his hand and then his lips found the softness of her breast she thought she must die or faint from too much sensation.

And as she was swept irresistibly into the vortex of his hands and voice and mouth, Christina knew that he had indeed claimed her soul, as he had once said he would. He had won everything, and tomorrow she would probably hate him again. Or wish she could. But tonight was past all redemption.

She was unaware of the hot tears sliding slowly down her face until he stilled. He raised himself slowly, one hand going to her face. For a long moment there was no sound between them. And then he swore viciously.

The sound was so unexpected that she jumped. The next thing she knew, he had withdrawn from her and stood up, and she felt as if all warmth and life had been denied her.

For a moment he stood with his back to her, breathing hard, and she lay there, bewildered, unsure what she had done wrong. Then she gathered the tatters of her courage as she pulled the sheets around her nakedness and sat up, reaching for him. "What is it?" she pleaded softly. "What have I done?"

He turned then, his face barely discernible in the darkness, and laughed. It was not a pleasant sound. "You? Nothing. I have been called a devil so long that it must indeed have gone to my head. I thought I could take you without conscience or regret, but I find I can't. Isn't that amusing?"

"What—what do you mean?" she made herself ask at last, dreading the answer.

"Nothing. Except the jest is on me this time, sweetheart. You see, I had thought to drag you down with me, but instead the boot's on the other leg. It would seem you have drawn me up, despite myself and all of my intentions."

"What?" she whispered in bewilderment.

"Never mind," he said roughly, reaching for the door. "Pray accept my apologies and assurances that such a thing will never happen again. I hope you and Charles will be very happy."

And he was gone on the words, leaving her to stare after him, then collapse onto her tumbled bed in a paroxysm of bitter laughter.

After that they maintained a scrupulous politeness toward one another when they chanced to meet, which was seldom. They were both at some pains to avoid the other, and it proved surprisingly easy in so small a house.

Christina woke the next morning with hollow eyes and the determination to banish Deveril from her mind and heart once and for all. And if that proved more difficult than she had hoped, she had her shame and the realization that she had had a very narrow escape to serve as a goad when she weakened.

And luckily Charles began to mend rapidly, as if he had passed some major hurdle. He required less of her time as a nurse and more to keep him occupied, for he complained of feeling bored the moment she was out of his sight.

But his recovery brought its own problems, for he was almost touchingly grateful to her and Deveril. It seemed not to occur to him that his best friend and his fiancée might have betrayed him during the long days and nights of being cooped up together, and that very naivete was somehow more painful than an outright accusation would have been. It was difficult to tell what Deveril was thinking, for she had to acknowledge to herself that she had never known that. But for herself Charles's trust was a constant reminder of her shame and betrayal.

But if she had thought it hard to hear Charles speak unendingly of her nobility and courage, that was nothing to what it cost her to hear him talk of their coming marriage as if it had never been in doubt. And once he was well enough he did so constantly, seeming not to notice her unnatural silence on the subject.

That was bad enough, but at least once he did so in Deveril's hearing. Christina flushed and then paled, expecting to find Deveril's mocking eyes on her and that well-known cynical twist to his mouth. But to her surprise he turned away abruptly and soon made an excuse to leave the room.

And after that she was forced to acknowledge that he was at considerably greater pains to avoid her than she had been to avoid him. The realization struck her painfully anew, opening wounds scarcely healed over as yet. But it soon became obvious that he could not stand to be long in the same room with her. Her entrance was his cue to rise and leave, no matter what he had been doing.

She accepted it bitterly, as she had accepted everything else. She had little concept of what had happened, except that for whatever reason he had found he could not go through with it. He had meant to seduce her to insure that Charles would not marry her, and when he had succeeded even better than he must have hoped, he had inexplicably drawn back. Perhaps he had found a conscience at last, as his last words seemed to have indicated, and discovered he could not so betray his oldest friend. Or perhaps he had merely proved what he had set out to, which was that he could have her whenever he chose and on whatever terms, and he had found the actual conquest not worth his effort.

In either case it little mattered. He had despised her from

the first and taken little pains to disguise the fact. And if she had fallen prey to his fatal fascination, despite every warning to the contrary, the more fool she.

But mostly she just longed to return to England and have the whole thing behind her. She was aware of a homesickness for her brother and her native land that she would not have thought possible.

Unfortunately, there had been no further word of the travelers. Robin had promised to return as quickly as possible, so she could only assume he had had to escort the party all the way back to London. Certainly the problem of money had begun to loom large in her consciousness, for it was possible Robin hadn't enough to pay for his return journey. And if so, she feared the next few weeks were going to be very unpleasant indeed.

Then something happened to overshadow even her present unhappiness and make her think she had been exceedingly naive to think that the worst must be over.

Chapter 20

CHRISTINA was just coming from Charles's room one morning when the landlady informed her she had two visitors below. She was astonished, for she knew no one in the district, and so said a little stupidly, "For me? Are you sure."

"But yes, Mademoiselle. They specifically asked for the English demoiselle."

Christina went downstairs, puzzled. Two men of respectable appearance looked up as she entered the coffee room and immediately came forward. She had never seen either of them before.

"Ah, *mademoiselle*," said one in pleasantly accented English. "We are sorry to disturb you, but we understand your brother is not here and hoped you might be able to help us. He was to have brought a small package into France with him—a small matter of some private letters. My friend and I are most eager to receive them. Did he perhaps leave them with you?"

She looked at them more closely, her earlier puzzlement over Robin's mysterious package slightly recurring. But they looked wholly unremarkable. "I am sorry you have had a wasted journey," she said apologetically and slightly embarrassed. "But I am afraid they were, er, lost overboard while we were crossing the Channel."

"Lost!" exclaimed the spokesman, looking thunderstruck.

"It was a—a—most unfortunate accident. Please accept my sincerest regret and that of my brother as well. They were important?"

"Not—important," he said, recovering a little. "But a matter of some sentimentality, you understand. You are sure there can be no mistake? Perhaps your brother took them with him. Where, if I may ask, has he gone?"

"He was obliged to go back to England. But unfortunately there can be no mistake."

The one who had yet to speak did not seem to like that, for he frowned heavily. The two exchanged some wordless message, and then the first said, a shade less politely, "I regret, but you understand we are anxious to regain the papers. Where may we locate your brother?"

She was becoming a little uneasy at this persistence. Unfortunately, Deveril was gone on a mysterious errand, as he seemed to do more frequently now that Charles was better, and Charles himself was still too weak to be of any use in an emergency. In a pinch she might call to the half-grown youth who looked after Madame's guests' horses. But he was undoubtedly out in the stables and not too bright either.

Then she told herself she was being foolish, imagining threats where none existed. But when she turned, she saw with a sense of shock that the second man had pulled out a pistol and was pointing it at her.

"You will take us both upstairs to your room, *mademoiselle*," said the first, still sounding absurdly calm under the circumstances, "and not call out. Is that understood?"

Christina's heart was clamoring in her chest by now, and

she began to long for Deveril's intimidating presence, whatever lay between them. "I—I—there must be some mistake," she insisted weakly.

"No mistake, unless it is your brother's. And now, *mademoiselle*—" The one with the pistol waved it toward the door, and the other came and took a firm grip on her arm. "Just in case there is any misunderstanding or you are tempted to call out to anyone. That would be most unfortunate, I regret to say."

Her legs were beginning to tremble in earnest, but she had no choice but to accompany them up the stairs to her bedchamber. Unfortunately, the landlady was nowhere in sight, and owing to their having taken over the whole house there were no other guests. The woman from the village now came only in the mornings, and had already gone home that day. Christina knew she was on her own.

She indicated her bedchamber reluctantly and entered as they held the door for her. It all seemed like a very bad dream, for Charles was just two doors away and all the healthy noises of dinner being prepared in the kitchens below rose clearly through the open windows.

The two men followed her and shut the door behind them. Then the one with the pistol motioned her to a chair and kept his pistol trained on her while the other began methodically to search her room.

She could only watch helplessly as he pulled out drawers and chests with little concern to neatness and dumped their contents on the floor. So far they had offered her no violence and she was thus not overly afraid—yet. But the problem of the contents of Robin's mysterious parcel was beginning to loom largely. She didn't know whether to regret or be relieved that it had been lost overboard.

At least she did not suspect this was merely another of Deveril's tricks. Deveril knew nothing of the package, and she had been suspicious of it from the first. "Robin, oh, Robin," she thought helplessly. "How could you?" It was no wonder he had behaved so oddly when he found out what had happened to it.

The intruders did not find what they were looking for. The one doing the searching finally exhausted drawers and wardrobes, and with an oath he turned his attention to the bed, dragging the bed coverings and mattress off. When he still found nothing he ripped open both mattress and pillows with a knife, scattering a mountain of feathers among the chemises and petticoats already littering the floor.

His companion, who seemed to be in charge, abruptly stopped him with a short word. The second abandoned his search, his temper by no means improved, and turned to Christina. "We are through with games, *mademoiselle*. Where is it? You would save yourself and your brother a great deal of unpleasantness if you told us now."

She swallowed, wondering a little hysterically if she should send them off on a false trail. But it seemed safest to stick to the truth, and so she said as calmly as she could manage, "I told you, the package was lost overboard the first day, along with all my baggage. You might have spared your-self—and me—all this unnecessary destruction."

He looked in disbelief, and she had to acknowledge that it was an incredible enough story. "Then where is your brother, *mademoiselle*?" he inquired again, all politeness gone from his tone.

She was instantly afraid for Robin. The papers—whatever they were—seemed unpleasantly important. Again she didn't like to speculate what they must have contained. "I told you, he has returned to England," she said with a bravado she was far from feeling. She suddenly hoped with all her heart that it was true, and Robin was not even then on his way back.

The one with the pistol swore violently, and again there

was an exchange of silent signals. Then the second calmly and dispassionately struck her across the face.

The blow was open-handed and not meant to do serious damage, but it was strong enough to throw her from her chair. She landed in a crumpled heap on the floor, her head ringing and her first reaction as much surprise as pain.

She might scream for help, of course, for it was apparent things had gone beyond simple misunderstanding. But one of the men was armed, and the only one likely to hear her would be Charles. Charles with one arm in a sling and still abominably weak from his near brush with death. Not only would he be of little use against them, but might do himself a great deal of damage in the attempt.

"Where is your brother, *mademoiselle*?" repeated the one who had hit her, making no attempt to help her up.

It was the last question he asked. Before she could gather her wits together to think what she was going to do, there was a brief knock at the door and then Deveril himself opened it without waiting for an answer.

"Christina, Madame DuBois told me you had—" he began without preamble, and then trailed to a stop at the scene before him.

One moment only they all stared at each other in horror, Christina still on the floor, the one intruder standing over her, half turned to stare at the newcomer, the other with his pistol wavering for a moment.

Then everything happened at once. Christina screamed Deveril's name in warning, the man beside her turned quickly back to silence her, and the one with a pistol made up his mind. But he was one second too late. With two swift blows Deveril had laid him on the floor, the pistol discharging harmlessly toward the ceiling.

It was a very different Deveril from any that Christina was yet familiar with. His eyes were murderous in his dark face, and Christina did not blame the other man for taking one look and making no attempt to rescue his fallen comrade. He abandoned her without a qualm and leapt for the open window, where he quickly disappeared over the sill.

The first seemed to come to the same conclusion, for he left his pistol and made for the door and the stairs, disappearing down them with equal rapidity.

Deveril made no attempt to go after either of them but came swiftly to Christina where she still lay and picked her up. "Are you hurt?" he demanded huskily.

"No. Oh, no. Only shaken. You came just in the nick of time."

"You are generous," he said harshly, putting up a hand to gently touch her bruised cheek. He still looked oddly murderous.

It was thus that Charles found them, interrupting whatever else might have been said between them. Sketchily attired in his dressing gown, he exploded into the room, only coming to a stop at the sight of his fiancée almost in the arms of his best friend and the room in chaos.

"What—I thought I heard a pistol! Good God, what on earth happened in here?" he demanded in astonishment. Then he saw her bruised cheek and added in horror, "My God, Christina!"

Deveril calmly released her and righted the chair for her, ignoring him. "We will get you some ice in a moment to lay on your cheek," he said, putting her into it. "Charles, I'm glad you're here. Go and fetch her some brandy."

She tried to protest, but she might have saved her breath. Charles, after a stunned instant, went hurriedly to do as he was bid, and Mme. DuBois and the maid, both liberally floured from their cooking, came plowing up the stairs in alarm to discover what had happened. When they saw the room they too stopped short, and the maid hastily crossed herself.

"Holy Mother!" cried the stout landlady, staring in horror at the shambles. "What has occurred?"

Deveril's steady hand on Christina's shoulder kept her from replying, though she was in no hurry to make explanations. "There would seem to have been a robbery which Mademoiselle Castleford interrupted," he explained briefly.

The landlady exclaimed at that, completely shocked that such a thing could have happened in so small a village, and her own inn. Especially in broad daylight. It was unheard of.

Christina did not need the continued pressure of Deveril's hand to let the falsehood go unchallenged. Mme. DuBois exclaimed for some minutes, too full of apologies for any awkward questions, while the maid was merely enjoying the unprecedented excitement.

But Charles returned all too soon with the brandy. Deveril took it from him and forced Christina to drink some of it, despite her protests. "Stop complaining and drink it," he said in his autocratic way. "You know it will do you good."

She weakly complied, using the time to gather her badly shattered wits. But she need not have worried. Deveril soon managed to dispatch the landlady back downstairs again, helped no doubt by the smell of something burning that began to permeate the house and sent Mme. DuBois off in alarm to rescue her dinner.

Charles was leaning against the door frame watching both Deveril and Christina, a slight frown in his eyes. When the landlady and maid had taken themselves off, he asked slowly, "*Was* it thieves? I agree with Madame DuBois. It seems devilish queer to me. In fact a good deal seems to be going on that I don't understand."

"You should be back in bed," said his lordship bluntly. "You'll suffer a relapse if you're not careful."

"No, let him stay." Christina sounded weary even to herself. "He—he has a right to know." She did not question how Deveril knew, but it seemed he did. Perhaps he was the devil, after all.

After a moment Deveril shrugged. "Very well, then. Did they find what they were after?"

She looked at him. "How did you guess?"

"It wasn't very hard."

She was by no means so convinced, but Charles demanded shortly, "Guess what? Find what? Would you mind very much explaining if I am indeed to be let in on the secret? I feel as if I have been ill for months, not a few weeks."

There was no time to wonder at his words. She hesitated, then unwillingly told them of the package that Robin had entrusted to her.

Charles looked astonished, but Deveril betrayed no surprise whatsoever. After a moment Charles asked him frankly, "Did you know, then? Did Robin tell you?"

"No. But I saw Robin hand his sister a package on the day we set out. I was, er, watching her rather carefully, you see," he said dryly. "That alone would have meant nothing, of course. But there had to be an explanation for that earlier holdup." He carefully did not look at Christina. "Ordinary footpads don't waste time searching through trunks unless they've been warned there's something valuable in one of them."

Christina flushed crimson, feeling ashamed as she had seldom felt in her life. It seemed she and Robin both were fools, for she had been as blind as he had.

"But—but this is incredible," Charles exploded. "What could possibly be in the package to warrant such extraordinary steps?"

That was the next question that had been haunting Christina. But Deveril answered indifferently, as if it scarcely mattered, "Almost anything, I imagine. Keep in mind that all traffic between England and France has been curtailed for many years."

"He said it was papers," offered Christina unwillingly. "It—you don't think it could have been something treasonous?"

"I would say it was most unlikely," answered Deveril at his most damping.

She was immensely grateful to him, if not wholly convinced by his unexpected kindness. She knew it was far more than she deserved. Charles looked less convinced, and demanded, as if only then rousing to the fact, "But are you saying those are the fellows who shot me?"

"Again, most unlikely. Did you recognize either of them, Miss Castleford?" When she shook her head, Deveril added, "At any rate, they now know we don't have what they're looking for. We shouldn't be troubled any further."

"You're damn cool," exclaimed Charles. "I must say, this is all outside my experience. What will they do, then?"

Christina was afraid she knew, and it terrified her. Robin might have been a fool, but she did not like to think of him hurrying back to rescue her, straight into the arms of his enemies.

But there was no time for Deveril to reassure her, if that was what he meant to do. They had remained in Christina's tumbled room, the door still open, oblivious to what was happening anywhere else in the house. But now they were forcibly jerked back to reality.

"Christina!" came a scandalized voice from the open doorway. "It's a good thing I decided to come and see for myself what you were up to!"

Chapter 21

CHRISTINA turned in somewhat of a daze, wholly unprepared for this latest disaster. "Grandmama!" she gasped in disbelief.

Barbara Foxcroft was exceedingly well preserved for her age and still showed signs of the great beauty that had captivated even a king in her day. If her hair no longer remained the red that nature had intended and her complexion showed the inevitable effect of her sixty-odd years, most of them lived to the hilt, she nevertheless contrived through a trick of supreme self-confidence to present the appearance of a woman a good deal younger.

She was dressed at the moment in an extremely expensive and becoming traveling dress, and was accompanied by an attractive middle-aged woman of far less modish appearance and more cheerful demeanor. For a moment Christina was in so much shock at seeing her grandmother she scarcely noticed the other woman.

"Aye, miss, you may well blush and protest," stated that formidable lady grimly, taking in the state of her granddaughter's room and her two companions. "This is a fine kettle of fish. Here have I come halfway across Europe to rescue you from a highly unsuitable match—though if you mean to hole up at an inn with him for more than a week with no sign of a chaperone, you can only thank your stars, my girl, if he does consent to marry you—only to find you in a compromising position with *two* men. Fine behavior, I must say.''

Charles had turned to take in this apparition with something like astonishment, but now he said stiffly, ''I am Charles Heybridge, ma'am. Her fiancé. And I can assure you there is no impropriety.''

She looked him up and down, plainly unimpressed with what she saw. ''Hmmph! As if you would know if there had been. And who the devil is this, then?'' she demanded, nodding toward Deveril.

''I think I can answer that,'' said the second lady somewhat surprisingly, though there was an engaging twinkle in her eye. ''Pray allow me to present my son, ma'am. Lord Deveril.''

Barbara Foxcroft eyed him, in no way taken aback. ''Oh, Deveril, is he?'' she asked, interested. ''Not that that makes it any better. In fact, a good deal worse, now that I recall his reputation.''

''Grandmama!'' cried Christina again, highly humiliated.

But Deveril had eyes only for his mother at the moment. ''Undoubtedly a good deal worse, ma'am,'' he acknowledged indifferently. ''Well, Mama?'' There was an answering hint of amusement in his own eyes, and a good deal of affection, and he took her hand and kissed it. ''Surely you too have not come halfway across Europe to save Charles from an ineligible match?''

Lady Deveril gave his hand a little squeeze, her face softening for a moment with love and more than a little mischief. ''Of course not, my love. Only I have had the *most* informative chat with your uncle, you know,'' she said mysteriously. ''And so when I met Mrs. Foxcroft quite by chance, I thought I would come and see for myself. I hope you aren't angry with me.''

He gazed down at her, looking very different from his usual sardonic self. "Oh, you have, have you?" he repeated, sounding unsurprised. "I suppose by now I should be used to your uncanny prescience.''

"My dear, it didn't take much prescience, I assure you," countered Lady Deveril, laughing up at him. "But you are making me forget my manners." She turned and charmingly held out her hand to a gaping Christina. "And you must be Miss Castleford," she said kindly. "I have been longing to meet you, my dear.''

"H-have you, ma'am?" stumbled Christina, taking Lady Deveril's hand and feeling a little as if she had suddenly gone mad. "I mean, that is very kind of you.''

"Nonsense, my dear," said that lady briskly, subjecting her to a thorough but kindly inspection. "And I must confess that having met you, I begin to understand at long last. Charles, my dear, shouldn't you be in bed?''

Christina was glad that the focus of attention shifted to Charles, since there seemed to be no answer to Lady Deveril's words. Charles was himself looking a little dazed, and the odd frown had come back into his eyes but he greeted Lady Deveril with obvious affection.

Barbara Foxcroft, never one to be left for long out of the conversation, interrupted in her autocratic way, "Never mind that. What in the devil has been going on here is what I demand to know. First we hear an unbelievable tale of murderous highwaymen in broad daylight—though come to that, I would believe anything of the French these days— and that this man my granddaughter has gotten herself engaged to has foolishly allowed himself to be wounded—''

"Grandmama!" interrupted Christina angrily. "He is

standing right here. And he hardly allowed himself to be wounded on purpose.''

She ignored that. ''And now we arrive to find my grand-daughter's room looking as if a cyclone had been through it. Perhaps, if you are indeed Deveril, you would be good enough to explain the meaning of all this to me?''

''I would be happy to, ma'am,'' responded his lordship coolly. ''But first, you say you heard of our mishap? From whom, may I ask?''

''Oh, didn't we tell you, dear?'' interrupted his mother cheerfully. ''We met dear Lucinda and that absurd Lady Danbury at Dover quite by chance. I have always thought her completely foolish, you know. She was still almost incoherent with fear when we met her, though I must confess it was hard to tell what had exercised her most: the fact that you were held up or that you had callously commandeered the coach for Charles's use and left them there to be murdered by returning brigands.''

Christina heard this with a leap of her heart. ''Was—was my brother with them, ma'am?'' she inquired anxiously.

''No, I believe he had already left them. Lucinda mentioned that he was most anxious to get to Brussels—but perhaps I have that wrong, since you are still here.''

Barbara Foxcroft, as usual, was not to be long put off. ''Never mind that,'' she said irritably again. ''I demand to know what has been going on here.''

Christina's heart sank, knowing that if her grandmother ever found out about Robin's latest escapade she would disown him forever. But it was Deveril who said easily, ''Merely a robbery attempt, ma'am. It need not concern you.''

''Hhmph,'' she said again, unimpressed. ''It seems to me there is a great deal too much of that going on in France these days, if you are to be believed, young man. And why this room, pray? My granddaughter has nothing of particular value to steal."

"I am afraid your guess is as good as mine. But I regret that at the moment I cannot remain and discuss it with you. I have, er, urgent business to attend to that will necessitate being absent for a couple of days." He turned again, his face softening. "In fact, Mama, I am delighted you are here, for I don't like to leave them unattended."

She took this in stride, evidently surprised at nothing her son might do. "Are you, dear?" she inquired sunnily. "Then I'm glad too."

It was Charles who demanded what Christina was longing to. "I don't understand any of this. Where are you going, Dev?"

"I expect you are feeling faint, dear," her ladyship assured him kindly. "You will be more the thing once you have gone back to bed."

Charles's lips twitched despite himself, and his lordship said surprisingly, "Mama, I adore you! I am sorry to be obliged to rush off like this, but I rely upon your good sense. Take care of Charles and, er, Miss Castleford for me, and prevent her from doing anything foolish if you can."

"Yes, dear. It will give us a chance to become better acquainted."

"Where the devil is he going?" complained Barbara Foxcroft, outraged. "I am beginning to think the whole world has run mad."

"Why, haven't you guessed?" inquired his lordship coolly, "To Brussels, of course."

Christina had only one more stolen moment with him before he left. He had gone coolly away to change and pack, leaving her to face her grandmother's irate questions and

Lady Deveril's amused acceptance. It was only when she had succeeded in countering these and arranged bedchambers for them both, then seen her grandmother, never a cheerful traveler, onto her bed while Lady Deveril saw to an exhausted Charles, that she was able to escape.

She found Deveril in the hall, already booted and in his driving coat, ready to set out. She ran up to him and cried breathlessly, "You are—I'm not mistaken that you are going to find Robin. Am I?"

He took her hands and drew her into the coffee room, away from prying ears. "If I can," he conceded. "I have no notion what good I may do—probably none. But he should undoubtedly be warned that his mysterious package has, er, taken on unexpected importance."

She almost shuddered. "Thank you. With you there I know—I know he will be safe. He—" She broke off, then added with difficulty, "I beg you to believe that there is no real vice in him, my lord. Whatever he has done, it was through carelessness and—and folly. He did not mean any harm to come of it."

His hands tightened a little on hers. "I assure you you need not defend him to me. Nevertheless he put you in considerable danger. It occurs to me it is time and more that young man grew up and began to face the consequences of his actions."

"I think he—has begun to do that by going to Brussels," she said earnestly. "He can only be trying to clear the matter up. I don't excuse what he did. I only came to thank you for what you are doing and for not telling my grandmother the truth."

He grimaced ruefully. "You must admit I am not used to hearing such words coming from you, my dear. I only hope I may justify this newfound confidence in me."

She dropped her eyes and suddenly seemed to recall her

hands still in his and tried to withdraw them. "If—if I have not always valued you as I ought, my lord," she said with difficulty, hardly knowing what she said, "you must know that after this afternoon I am hopelessly in your debt. I don't know why you did what you did, especially after all that has been between us. But I shall never forget it. Never."

"Don't overwhelm me with too much civility all at once, Red, I beg you," he said in amusement. "I must go. When I get back will be time enough to tally the reckoning between us. You know that has yet to be done, don't you? But I know I leave you in good hands. I think you will like my mother."

"Oh, yes, how could I not?" she said foolishly. Now that the time had come she was strangely loath to let him go. "But you will be careful, won't you?"

He smiled, raised her hands to his lips, and lightly kissed them. "Don't you know the devil looks after his own, my sweet? And that he always gets what he wants."

The next moment he was gone. She stood at the window staring foolishly after him. Her hands were at her hot cheeks, and she was trying desperately to remind herself of the inseparable gulf that lay between them.

Christina, thus left alone with her two unlikely duennas, did not much enjoy the next several days.

Lady Deveril was exceedingly kind, but it seemed to an embarrassed Christina that his lordship's mother was enjoying a private jest of some sort. Certainly she displayed a flattering interest in Christina, a surprising tolerance toward her grandmother, and seemed neither shocked nor very interested in her son's oldest friend's betrothal. In fact, once when Barbara Foxcroft was animadverting bitterly against it out of Charles's hearing, she said blithely, "Oh, as to that, I wouldn't worry too much, ma'am. After all, they aren't married yet."

Barbara Foxcroft looked at her sharply and unexpectedly closed her lips. Only Christina had flushed crimson, thinking that at least in opposition to the marriage her ladyship took after her formidable son.

If so, it was the only one. She frankly mothered Charles, who seemed to take it very much for granted, and showed herself not the least high in the instep. She seemed never above her company or dissatisfied with the primitive accommodations, kept even Barbara Foxcroft in a relatively pleasant mood, and all in all managed to keep a very disparate party on surprisingly pleasant terms.

Christina, liking her very much, still tried to spend as little time in her company as possible. The circumstances of their meeting, her grandmother's reputation, and her own very uneven relationship with Deveril all seemed to combine to make the present intimacy between them doubly humiliating, and she could not be at her ease in Lady Deveril's presence.

But if she was able to prevent any uncomfortable tête-à-têtes with a puzzled Lady Deveril, she had no hope, of course, of avoiding her grandmother. Barbara Foxcroft cornered her shortly after she arrived and fixed her bright, fierce gaze upon her. "Well, Miss," she grated, "a fine kettle of fish, I must say. What have you to say for yourself?"

"Not a thing, Grandmama," said Christina wearily. "What do you expect me to say?"

Surprisingly, that seemed to mollify the old woman somewhat. "That, at least, doesn't surprise me," she barked. "A fine muddle you've made of everything. *And* of my plans, I might add. Though it might have been worse," she added even more surprisingly. "Young Heybridge seems a personable enough boy, I grant you that. His fortune's no more than respectable, and you're a fool, for you might have done much better for yourself. Very much better. But I fear now you've no choice but to marry him."

While Christina was still trying to adjust to this unlooked-for leniency, her grandmother struck. "Unless, of course, you can bring Deveril up to scratch. And don't waste your breath telling me there's nothing between you. I've eyes in my head, haven't I? Well, speak up, girl! Did he seduce you?" she added outrageously.

"No, he did not!"

"Hmmm. In that case you're a fool, girl. Especially since this fiancé of yours must needs get himself wounded and leave the pair of you together in an intimacy that would try the control of a saint. Which Deveril is not, I'll warrant. Are you in love with him?"

"I will remind you, ma'am, that I am betrothed to Charles Heybridge," said Christina stiffly.

"Then the more fool you," retorted her grandmother bluntly. "At any rate, engagements were made to be broken, as Lady Deveril says. Bah, what an age it is. I should have seen to your upbringing myself, for you've not the least notion how to bring the thing off. He's an attractive devil, that I will grant you, however high-handed and however bad his reputation may be. In my day, I can tell you, I'd have had a declaration from him long since."

Christina raised her head and met her grandmother's eyes without flinching. "But of what sort, Grandmama?" she demanded bitterly. "I have no doubt that Lord Deveril would have been happy enough to take me for his mistress. Should I have accepted him?"

"Don't take me up, so, Missy! Though I still maintain if you'd been clever you might have forced his hand. The situation could hardly have been more advantageous, locked in a remote inn together for more than a fortnight. But I repeat, modern girls don't know how to seize their opportunities."

"Then perhaps I should tell you, ma'am, that for most

of our acquaintance his lordship has done his utmost to prevent my marriage to his best friend—not out of jealousy, but dislike for my background. Believe me, he is highly unlikely to offer me any respectable connection, even to avoid a scandal. Good God, his whole reputation has been one scandal after another! Not even you will succeed in forcing him to wed the granddaughter of Barbara Foxcroft. And if you could, I would rather remain single and penniless for the rest of my days than wed under such terms. Have I made myself very clear?''

Her voice had risen at the last, until she was fairly shouting. She knew she had overreacted, but the last thing she wanted was for her grandmother to try to force a declaration from Deveril. She thought she would die first.

"Very well," grumbled her grandmother, apparently willing to drop the subject for the moment. But there was still a speculative gleam in her eye.

Christina mistrusted her, but thought that since she had taken the bull by the horns, it would be better to prepare her grandmother for the worst. "And as for Charles, perhaps I should warn you that I am by no means still convinced we should suit," she added deliberately.

But her grandmother reacted to that in predictable outrage. "Suit? *Suit?*" she cried. "By God, spare me from the present namby-pamby age. Well, all I can say, my girl, is that you'd better marry one or the other of 'em, and that quickly. You have spent a fortnight in Deveril's pocket with no other chaperone but a badly wounded man, and you're right that his reputation guarantees few will believe it was innocent. If Deveril won't marry you, then you'd better hope to God Heybridge will, though if he's eyes in his head he'll have seen the truth himself by now. And that's all I have to say on the subject.''

Chapter 22

HER CONVERSATION with her grandmother was bad enough, as far as Christina was concerned, but a later chat with Lady Deveril was far worse. Christina had come impetuously into Charles's bedchamber to speak with him one morning, only to find Lady Deveril alone there, placidly engaged in her embroidery.

Christina checked on the doorstep, an unwilling heat touching her cheeks. "Oh, I beg your pardon, ma'am. But where is Charles?"

"Gone to try out his wobbly legs, or so he says, poor boy. Whenever I have been laid up in bed for any length of time, I know I can't wait to be up and about. My son would undoubtedly say it is because I tend to so many people's business other than my own. No, don't go, my dear," she added as Christina made to withdraw. "I don't know how it is, but we never seem to have an opportunity for a private chat."

Christine came in and sat down, hoping Lady Deveril did not notice her reluctance. "Did you wish to say something to me, ma'am?"

"Why, not in particular, my dear. But since you are going to be part of the family—"

Christina's head jerked up in shock. "Part of the family—?" she blurted.

"In a manner of speaking, I mean, for you must know I think of Charles as another son," finished that lady blithely, seemingly unaware of the consternation she had caused. "He is such a sweet boy."

"I—who? Charles?" This was worse and worse. Christina knew she was making an utter fool of herself.

"Of course. Who else would I mean?"

Christina could take little more of this and so decided to cut through the fencing. "Do you object to the match, ma'am?" she asked directly. "Is that what this is about?"

"My dear, Charles is a grown man," answered Lady Deveril, amusement in her eyes. "I wouldn't presume to judge what will suit him or not."

"Your son did," said Christina bitterly. "You must know that he has done everything in his power to bring an end to the betrothal."

"Ah." For some reason the laughter in Lady Deveril's eyes had increased. "You mustn't think I don't value my son as I ought, my dear, but Deveril is sometimes inclined to be . . . uncompromising in his views. He also possesses an unpleasant reputation—encouraged by himself, I fear, for some absurd reason I've never been able to understand. But the truth is that once he gives his affections, no one can be more loyal or more charmingly generous. I should know. I could give you a hundred instances of his care for me and those few he loves. But then I fear I should sound like nothing so much as a doting parent, which I have always thought a bore."

"I daresay he did what he did out of loyalty to Charles," agreed Christina in a dull voice.

"Charles?" Lady Deveril seemed surprised. "Why, of

course I meant him too. After all, they have been friends since they were in short coats, you know.''

Christina found she could not resist turning the screw to her own torture. ''And, then too, they will be brothers soon enough in reality, I understand. I mean when he marries Miss Heybridge.''

''Lucinda?'' repeated Lady Deveril in the liveliest astonishment. ''But my dear, he doesn't mean to marry Lucinda. Did you think he did?''

Christina turned toward her slowly. ''He seemed—that is, they seemed so close. And he showed toward her a gentleness—a protectiveness—that seemed to indicate—I mean—''

Lady Deveril took pity on her. ''My dear, I have learned to place very little reliance on my ability to predict my son's behavior, but I would be very surprised indeed if he were to offer for Lucinda Heybridge. His taste is very much otherwise. Didn't you know?''

''How could I, ma'am? If you are thinking—if you have been listening to my grandmother,'' said Christina with great difficulty, wishing she had never embarked on this conversation, ''you must know it is all absurd. At any rate Deveril despises me.''

''Does he, my dear?'' asked her ladyship dryly. ''May I ask you an impertinent question? Are you in love with Charles?''

Christina abruptly rose and took an agitated turn about the room, her cheeks crimson. ''I don't know,'' she admitted at last, shamefaced. ''He fell in love with me, you see—or I thought he did. And he was charming and kind and seemed to have everything I so desperately wanted. Oh, that sounds awful. But I meant to make him a good wife, I promise you, ma'am.''

''And now?''

''I don't know. I don't seem to know anything any longer.

I had made up my mind not to go through with it after all but my grandmother tells me I have placed myself in the position that I must marry him or see my reputation ruined— what little I possess, that is. But now I am no longer certain I am being fair to Charles. Deveril seems to think—to feel— that he only offered for me out of pity," she added unhappily. "And now, of course, he cannot in honor draw back. But I could. And lately—these past few days—I have begun to wonder if he, too, is beginning to have second thoughts. I beg you to advise me, ma'am. Will I be ruining Charles by wedding him?"

Lady Deveril folded up her embroidery and rose. "My dear," she said gently, "I have always thought that to give advice was exceedingly presumptuous. But I have a piece for you if you will listen to it. Do exactly as your heart dictates. Any man worth his salt will not care a fig who your grandmother was, or what her reputation might have been."

"And could you say that if it were in truth your son we were talking about?" demanded Christina bitterly.

Lady Deveril's mouth quirked as if again in amusement at some private jest. "With all my heart," she assured her. "But it seems to me you are avoiding the real problem, my dear. Once you face that, your answer will be easy. If you love Charles, then by all means wed him and tell the rest of the world to go to the devil. You see that I have spent too many years around my son and picked up his vocabulary, I fear. But if you don't, you may find yourself in hell instead. And no worldly gain can be worth that, believe me."

It was four interminable days before Deveril returned. Four days in which Christina had ample time to imagine the worst concerning her brother, listen to her grandmother's grumblings and bitter accusations, and try to maintain a cheerful face before Lady Deveril and Charles. It was an exhausting four days.

But when at last Deveril returned, he did it in his typical dramatic way. One moment the four of them were gathered in Charles's room in various stages of discontent and growing impatience. The next he had appeared in the doorway, still booted and greatcoated, although none of them had heard him arrive.

Charles was the first to notice him. He was now recovered enough to be up and dressed, though one arm reposed in a sling and he still tired easily. He had been oddly thoughtful over the last few days, but otherwise seemed in good enough spirits.

He had been laughingly teasing Christina about her inattention to the card game they were playing when he looked up and broke off to exclaim, "Dev! When did you get back?"

"Just now," said Deveril, regarding this exceedingly domestic scene with apparent amusement. "You seem much improved."

"Oh, Lord, yes. Almost as good as new. But what the devil have you been up to?"

"I'll tell you later," said his lordship. "Mama. Ma'am. You both seem to have made yourselves at home."

"And why shouldn't we?" demanded Barbara Foxcroft, in one of her petulant moods. "It's about time you bothered to return."

Deveril's eyes had not yet strayed to Christina, but she had stumbled to her feet at the first sound of his voice, the cards in her hand tumbling heedlessly to the floor. Before she could prevent herself she had gone to him, one question uppermost in her mind.

To her surprise and the evident interest of the remainder of the party he took both her hands warmly in his own, though his eyes held a warning and he said merely, "Miss Castleford. You are well, I trust?"

She flushed, belatedly aware of her folly and tried to withdraw her hands. "Oh, yes. Yes, of course. Your—your errand. Did it go . . . well?"

He pressed her hands one last time and almost reluctantly let them go. "Quite well, thank you," he answered politely. "If you care to hear about it, I will discuss it with you later, when I have had a chance to change out of all my dirt."

"Hmph! You might have done that before, if this is all the greeting and apology you have for us," complained Christina's grandmother, nevertheless a highly interested spectator to this byplay.

"Never mind that," said Charles. "Only tell us, what the devil have you been up to, Blaise? I don't mean to complain, for you left me admirably fixed, you know, with three such charming ladies to look after me. But you must admit your sudden disappearance was provokingly mysterious."

"I will admit only that it was distressingly tedious," answered Deveril in his most bored tone. "But I will come and tell you all about it once I have changed. Mama? I trust you have been enjoying yourself?"

That lady laughed deliciously. "Wretched boy! You know me too well, I fear. And how could I not, with such delightful company?"

But he seemed scarcely to be attending her. "I am glad to hear it. Miss Castleford, if you could spare me a few minutes, say in an hour's time? I have some news on that piece of business we discussed if you would care to hear it."

"Yes. Yes, of course," whispered Christina, fearing by his grim face what his news must be.

She was so overwhelmed with fear for Robin—for why else hadn't he returned himself?—that she underestimated her grandmother yet again.

"Just a moment, my lord," said that autocratic lady, straightening with a martial light in her eye. "I am less than reassured by what has been going on around here. Especially your conduct, if you must know."

"Grandmama!" cried Christina, appalled.

"None of your missishness, girl! Deveril knows I speak my mind. And I don't scruple to tell him to his face that he would do far better not to mistake me for a fool."

"That is the last thing I take you for, ma'am," said Deveril, his eyes taking on a dangerous silver cast.

"Hmm. Well, you would be well advised not to." Barbara Foxcroft did not miss the warning in those eyes or make the mistake of underestimating it. But she was, as she said, by no means a fool. "And I think you will agree it is past time for a frank discussion between us. I trust I make myself clear?"

"Grandmama!" cried Christina, crimson now with shame. "I forbid you to say another word. Do you hear me? I forbid you!"

"Oh, you do, do you?" snorted her grandmother. "Take care I don't wash my hands of you completely, my girl."

Lady Deveril was looking deliberately vague, but Charles had been looking between Christina's flushed countenance and Deveril's impassive one, and now said in a hard voice that was unlike him, "Just what exactly are you implying, ma'am?"

Barbara Foxcroft gave a rude laugh. "Implying? I am implying nothing. If *you* are happy with what went on here while you were ill, then who am I to complain?"

It was like a nightmare that Christina seemed powerless to end. She had known that her grandmother was capable of trying to force Deveril's hand, but now that it was happening it was somehow far worse and more humiliating than even she had anticipated. Charles was looking more than a little grim, and Deveril at his most unpleasant. Only Barbara Foxcroft looked mildly pleased with the effect she had created.

But after a horrible moment rescue came from an unexpected quarter. Charles drew in a deep breath, looking again between Christina's crimson face and Deveril's coldly unrevealing one. Then he said calmly, "You will excuse me, ma'am, but I think this matter is my concern, not yours. If Deveril has any explanations to make, it is to me and me alone. And now, if you don't mind, I am feeling a little tired. Perhaps you will all excuse me?"

And for once Barbara Foxcroft seemed to find herself outmaneuvered. She opened her mouth to say something else, then thought better of it. "Oh, you do, do you?" she exclaimed disrespectfully, hauling herself to her feet. "In that case I'll leave you to it. Though I confess I'd give much to be a fly on the wall for the next half hour. If nothing else, Deveril's so-called explanations should prove highly entertaining."

Christina waited for no one else but fled to her bedchamber, wholly unable to meet anyone's eyes.

It was fully an hour later when someone tapped briefly on her door. She made no answer, far too ashamed to want to talk to anyone. But after a moment the door opened anyway, and she heard a booted step on the floor inside her room.

She turned slowly, only to freeze at the sight of Deveril once more apparently ready for travel, for he was again wearing his greatcoat and held his hat, whip, and gloves in one hand.

"Are you leaving?" she asked dully, wholly unsurprised.

He took in her disheveled state and shamed eyes, but said

merely, in his cool voice, "I am taking you to see your brother. You will need nothing but your cloak, for he is at an inn not far from here. You will be back before you are missed."

She started up, her mind full of questions, her own distress for the moment forgotten. But after a moment she wordlessly allowed herself to be wrapped in her cloak and bundled out to his waiting phaeton.

She scarcely noticed the stable boy at the chestnuts' heads or his lordship's groom. Or that for some reason his lordship had not yet had his boxes taken down after his journey. Once they had set out she asked painfully, "Robin, is he—?"

"Alive and well, Red. There is no reason for you to look like that." For some reason Deveril had shaken off his earlier impassiveness and seemed extraordinarily calm.

Her eyes flew up to his, unable to take in his words for the moment. When she did, she whispered, "Oh, thank God," and promptly disgraced herself by bursting into tears.

With admirable calm he thrust a handkerchief into her hands and waited until she showed signs of regaining control. "If you don't stop crying soon, you will scare the horses," he remarked mildly.

She gasped and gave a watery laugh, as he had no doubt intended; then she obediently used the handkerchief to good effect. "In that case I beg your pardon. But Robin—? What—?"

"All in good time. We will be there shortly, and then you can ask me anything you like."

Since he seemed reluctant to talk in front of his groom, she could only subside, curbing her growing impatience. Now that the storm had passed, it occurred to her to wonder why Robin was holed up at a strange inn and had not simply returned with Deveril, and so her fears were not wholly allayed. But perhaps he wished to avoid their grandmother, which she could very well understand. She thought for herself she had no wish ever to lay eyes on her again.

They had been traveling less than an hour when Deveril pulled up before another modest inn, slightly more prosperous than the one they were presently occupying but by no means on a main road. The landlord seemed to have been waiting for them, for he hurried out immediately, welcoming Deveril and urging him to bring the lady in, for there was a sharp wind blowing that evening.

"Everything has been seen to as you requested, milord," he assured him with Gallic pleasure. "A fire has been lit in the best parlor against your coming, and the gentleman is waiting for you."

It was all so respectable and mundane that Christina was once more thrown. She had been bracing herself for some clandestine meeting with her brother, outlawed or in hiding for his life. This cheerful inn with its bowing and smiling host seemed almost unreal by comparison.

The landlord himself escorted them to a cheerful parlor where a fire burned in the grate and a bottle of wine and glasses stood ready. There was no sign of Robin.

As if unaware of her questions, Deveril went calmly to pour out a glass and handed it to her. "You look tired," he pronounced unexpectedly, as if looking at her for the first time. "Have you spent the last few days imagining who knows what horrors concerning your brother?"

She sipped a little of the wine, since it seemed easier than refusing it. "Only in my weakest moments," she admitted. "Where is Robin, sir?"

"In a moment." He poured out a second glass for himself and took a leisurely sip. "How did you get on with my mother, by the by? She seemed to have taken you under her wing, but then I could have predicted that. She has a notoriously soft heart."

"She is very kind," she said distractedly. "Had Robin discovered—?"

"All in good time, Red," he said amazingly, sounding merely amused. "Only tell me this first. Are you still determined to wed Charles?"

This was back to the same old argument, and she knew she no longer had any stomach for it. "Please," she said with difficulty, "it does no good—"

"It might do a very great deal of good," he interrupted calmly. "You accused me once of jumping to unfair conclusions. So now I am asking you, why did you become betrothed to a man you knew you weren't in love with?"

Chapter 23

"I THOUGHT you knew why," Christina answered wearily, her voice betraying her bitterness. "I did it for his money, of course."

"I'll admit I did think that at first," Deveril conceded. "I no longer do, if that means anything to you. Was it the security?" He sounded oddly very gentle.

She had no desire to go over the whole again, but perhaps she owed him that at least. "I can't expect you to understand," she said at last. "I know it must sound odd to you, but I fear there has been precious little of that in my life to date. My grandmother—well, you know everything there is to know about my grandmother. And my own mother was scarcely any more respectable or responsible, despite her more conventional marriage. Robin and I—but what is the use? Except that I used to dream of a conventional home and family, no matter how modest, and the simple assurance that it would not all be swept away from me tomorrow. Robin has reacted differently, for he seems to care no more for respectability than Grandmother does. But I sometimes think I would give up everything for the acceptance and belonging that you despise and flaunt so much."

Then she drew a breath and added quietly, "And you're

wrong, you know. I do . . . care for Charles. He was immensely kind when few others were, and I shall always be grateful to him.''

''Kind! Yes, he has always picked up strays and misfits, but that is hardly a basis for marriage. And what happens when he grows weary of his role as knight errant, as he always has in the past? That seems to me about as poor a reason for marriage as your milky gratitude.'' He sounded amused once more.

She was deeply hurt but refused to let him see that he had succeeded in wounding her. ''Your attitude is already well known to me, my lord. I hardly need to be reminded of it.''

''Is it? Then you would not make such mutton-headed statements to me, or talk about your *gratitude* to Charles. You little fool, I begin to think your longing for security has permanently addled your brain, for you are not stupid in the normal course of events. Do you know why I have opposed your marriage to Charles so strongly from the beginning?''

She stared at him, her cheeks crimson and her eyes bewildered. ''You made little secret of that, my lord, as I recall.''

''I said you were not ordinarily stupid. Has it never occurred to you that I have gone to extraordinary lengths to prevent a marriage that has very little to do with me?''

''You—Charles is your best friend.'' She faltered. ''You naturally did not care to—''

''God give me strength!'' He abruptly grasped her wrist and pulled her up to stand close beside him. Nor did he release his grip on her wrist. ''Your suspicions were correct from the beginning, Red. I wanted you myself.''

She drew a deep breath. ''That—that is something we will both of us get over, in time, my lord. It—all means nothing.''

''Doesn't it?'' he asked with a crooked grin. ''You little wetgoose, don't prattle hypocricies to me—you of all people.

Are we to meet, then, in polite company, you my best friend's wife, and make inane conversation to each other?''

She abruptly tried to release her wrist. "I don't—it doesn't—oh, why are you doing this?'' she demanded vexedly.

"This is why. Did you doubt it?'' And then he was kissing her hungrily as if he had long starved for the taste of her.

She was too weak not to surrender for a few moments to what she most desired in all the world, but she was the first to come down to earth. "Don't, please. We mustn't—'' Then, as reality gradually intruded, she wrenched herself from his arms and put the width of the room safely between them.

"This is because of my grandmother, isn't it?'' she demanded bitterly.

He was breathing a little fast as well, but seemed content, for the moment, to let her go. "Only indirectly.''

"I know she tried to force you to marry me, but you may believe, my lord, that nothing—''

"Rest easy, Red,'' he interrupted indifferently. "Nothing your grandmother could do would force me into offering for you.''

As a blow, it was as painful as it was unexpected. She flinched as if he had physically struck her, then looked around, seeing everything in a new light. "Robin isn't here, is he?'' she asked slowly at last. "This was all a trick.''

He shrugged, watching her face. "No.''

She could not believe she could have been such a fool. "I begin to understand. It's no wonder you were so unconcerned at my grandmother's transparent maneuverings. You had this in mind all the time, didn't you?''

"Your grandmother is a cursed nuisance, my dear,'' he admitted frankly. "In fact, she came close to wrecking all my plans.''

"And so you abducted me? But then, after all, you did warn me that you would stop at nothing to get your way, didn't you?"

He was untouched, as he had always been, by her contempt. "I did. It would have been well if you had remembered it, for it would have saved us both a good deal of grief."

"And so, to stop my marrying Charles and my grandmother's pathetic schemes, you will ruin me? Is that what you intend?" she challenged incredulously.

He shrugged. "I am vain enough to hope you will not find it that, my dear. But then I also warned you, did I not, that when I returned, it would be time to tally the reckoning between us. Come here."

When she made no move to do so, he added, again sounding merely amused, "No? Then I will come to you— for the last time. You know nothing will save you this time, don't you? Not my conscience or your pleading or this bread-and-water affection you feel toward Charles. I will show you no mercy."

She looked into his face and saw nothing but implacable purpose there. She thought now that she had never known him at all. But she also saw that this time there would indeed be no escape for her. "No," she whispered, ashamed. But instead of despair she was suddenly aware that a wild thrum of unworthy excitement was rising within her. It sickened her, but there seemed nothing she could do about it.

And he, devil that he was, knew it. His wicked eyes were triumphant, and a slow, slumbrous smile touched his lips. "And now you must make the running, my dear," he drawled. "I promised that I would bring you down to hell with me, but you must come of your own volition. You understand that, don't you?"

"Yes." He was right. He had won. She could no longer

fight him, for she realized that she had never been fighting him but only herself.

He waited patiently, for she knew he would do nothing to ease the passage for her, or force her hand. She must take the next ruinous steps all on her own.

She took one step and then another, mesmerized as she had always been by his remarkable silver eyes. When she finally reached him, she laid one trembling hand against his cheek.

Still he did not move. "Say it," he ordered.

She did not need to ask what he wanted, but she balked at that. It seemed he would leave her no pride at all.

Suddenly he gripped her hand, his grasp cruel. "Say it!" he rasped. "I warned you there would be no half measures. You must come all the way yourself. Now say it!"

Her eyes flew up to his, and suddenly it was easy to say, as if she had torn herself in two for so long for no reason. "I love you," she said, hating him, loving him. "Damn you, did you ever doubt it?"

She was surprised when a shudder took him, and he closed his eyes as if he were in pain. Then his hand softened on hers and he turned it to his mouth. "No. I never doubted it. But I feared that damnable pride of yours."

She had come too far to hold back now. "I have no pride where you are concerned. I never have. I sometimes think you are the devil, for I have no defenses against you," she whispered.

But he had suddenly swept her into his arms. She closed her eyes and made no demur when he began to kiss her. All her doubts, all her fears and pain, were useless to her now. There would never be any going back.

She endured his kisses, returning them with interest, all restraint gone. There was violence in the joining of their mouths, and hunger and triumph and pain. There was mindless joy and a wild blending of the mixed emotions of hate and love that had been between them.

Christina was beyond thought when Deveril pulled his mouth away and held her head between his hands, staring pantingly down at her, the triumph in his gaze obvious. "And Charles?" he demanded.

It was as if she must swim up from a long distance even to hear him. "Charles?" she repeated stupidly.

He laughed triumphantly. "God, Red. I have waited a long time to hear you say that."

Abruptly, as once a long time before, he pulled himself away and put the length of the room between them. She blinked foolishly after him, her wits still too drugged with passion to understand.

At last he turned, apparently in control of himself once more. "Charming as you look at the moment, my love, I fear we have much to do."

"Do?" she repeated still more stupidly.

"Yes, do." He was suddenly filled with an immense energy. "Don't look at me like that, or I fear we will be eternally delayed. And the priest downstairs is likely to take a rather dim view of that before the wedding."

"Wedding—?" she repeated stunned. "Is this some kind of horrible jest? I don't understand."

"That has been patently obvious from the first, my foolish Red," he said in amusement.

"You are not abducting me?"

"I have abducted you, and very satisfactorily too," he countered, his eyes again resting on her swollen mouth. "But much as some might equate being married to me as being married to the devil, I have hopes you will find it very much to your liking."

"But—but why?" she found herself crying in bewilderment.

"Why am I marrying you, or why have I eloped with you? The first I imagine must be painfully obvious. I have fallen in love with you, you little fool. You have succeeded in getting under my skin in a way I thought no woman would ever do."

None of it yet seemed real. "Then why—?"

"Have I abducted you? Because your grandmother came close to ruining all my plans. I am sorry to speak ill of your relations, my love, and in point of fact she is a remarkable old woman. I have great respect for her. But since she is exceedingly shrewd as well and could obviously see what we were so desperately trying to hide, I had every fear she would try to force my hand. And knowing that damnable pride of yours, I strongly suspected it would merely make you cling all the more to Charles, even though marrying him would have made both of you miserable."

"Charles!" she gasped, suddenly remembering. "Oh, God, I had forgotten him."

"You needn't worry, my love. Charles and I had a long talk before we left. He knows where you are and we have his blessing. In fact, he had begun to cherish suspicions about us some time ago."

"He did? And he doesn't mind?"

His lordship grinned in a way she was only becoming used to seeing in him. "If you want the unflattering truth, my love, I warned you Charles's passions seldom lasted long. At any rate, I think he is far more delighted at the prospect of seeing me caught in your toils than he ever was in marrying you himself. You need not fear he is nursing a broken heart."

"And—and your mother?" she asked, even more fearfully.

"We also had a brief talk before I left. She sent you her love and wanted me to remind you to follow your heart and let the rest of the world go to the devil. My mother's advice, by the way, is almost always excellent. I should also perhaps warn you, my love, that she has an uncanny and sometimes disconcerting habit of guessing what you would most want to hide. She has known the true state of affairs between us for a long time. Why else do you think she came?''

But that had brought another thought to mind. ''Good God, Robin!'' she cried guiltily. ''How could I forget him?''

''Perhaps you had something more pressing on your mind,'' he said unsteadily, an unholy gleam in his eyes. ''But very well, if we must. Robin also sends you his love and says I am to tell you he won the bet with himself. I take it he also guessed long ago what was between us? I found him, by the way, very much enjoying himself in Brussels. He assures me that the mysterious papers were not, as we so unjustly suspected, treasonous documents destined for Napoleon, but merely concerned some proposed business that was questionable, if not wholly illegal. He took the precaution of having read them, and so was able to satisfy our, er, importunate friends. They were, as you may have already realized, remarkably clumsy in their efforts to regain their documents. I believe Robin when he says they were far too ineffectual to have been government spies.''

She almost sagged with relief. ''Oh, thank God. I feared—''

''I know what you feared. For that I will not soon forgive your graceless young brother, my dear; not to mention it was ultimately his fault Charles was wounded. I think, if you don't mind, that he needs some interest to occupy him. I have offered to buy him a pair of colors and he has accepted. The military in peacetime should satisfy his love of adventure, and in addition a hussar uniform will become him admirably. I left him contemplating his transformation from private citizen philosophically, if not with great joy.''

''Yes, oh yes!'' she said gratefully. ''I have long begged Grandmother to do something like that.'' Then she added unwillingly, "But I fear she will be insufferable now. She will think this was all her doing, you know."

Deveril laughed. "Let her think so. But you still have not said you will marry me."

She was surprised that he would think he needed an answer, for she feared she had been transparently obvious. But now she said, just to punish him a little for all he had put her through, "Are you saying I have any choice in the matter?"

"Very little. But I want to hear the words."

Suddenly she was breathless again, for the levity had gone from his voice and face. She resisted for a heartbeat, then said weakly, "You were right from the beginning. However hard I have resisted I have not been able to escape my own heart. I had long ago decided I could not marry Charles."

He was once more laughing down at her with his devilish eyes. "At last. I told you long ago that we were two sides to the same coin, the Devil and his mate. But I fear my vanity was such that I needed to prove your love for me. Had I merely offered my hand and fortune in the conventional way, I would never have known whether you really preferred me to Charles or merely saw me as the better bargain. This way I have no doubts."

"Then this was all designed as a—oh, you are detestable! You are a—"

"Devil?" He laughed and pressed a kiss on the top of her curls. "I am content to burn in eternal hellfire, but only if you will do so with me. My darling, don't you know that I adore you?"

She lifted her face and let him set about proving it most admirably, letting the priest wait.